VOICE OF THE CONQUEROR

Borgo Press Books by JOHN RUSSELL FEARN

VOICE OF THE CONQUEROR

A CLASSIC SCIENCE FICTION NOVEL

JOHN RUSSELL FEARN

THE BORGO PRESS

MMXII

VOICE OF THE CONQUEROR

FIRST BORGO PRESS EDITION

Published by Wildside Press LLC

www.wildsidebooks.com

DEDICATION

To the memory of Robert Simms

CONTENTS

INTRODUCTION

by PHILIP HARBOTTLE

Although English writer John Russell Fearn died in 1960, his work continues to be reprinted worldwide. In recent years, more than a hundred of his novels in all genres have been returned to print, ensuring that his stories will continue to appear through the twenty-first century in various forms. This has been achieved despite the carping and continued bafflement of some literary critics, who cannot recognize the secret of his enduring appeal. It is a secret shared by several prolific novelists, such as the legendary Edgar Wallace. Quite simply, Fearn was a storyteller.

As writer Michael Gilbert has pointed out, Wallace—like Fearn—"was a storyteller who had learned, or maybe he knew by instinct, the first secret of story-telling. Something must be happening all the time. Not occurring haphazard, but happening in a consecutive and comprehensible chain of causation, to the resourceful hero and the attractive heroine who have been the protagonists of all real stories since storytelling began." Despite most of their stories having been written very swiftly, writers like Fearn and Wallace, as Gilbert observed, give the feeling that the author knew "that he had been seized of a good idea, exactly suited to his scope and talents, and that he was on the top of his form."

In England, Fearn is known not just as a science fiction author, but as a writer of detective stories and westerns. However, in the USA until recently, Fearn was still best known as a pioneer writer of science fiction, mainly because he began his career in the well-remembered and collectable prewar American pulp sf magazines, such as *Amazing Stories* and *Astounding Stories*. Wildside Press has republished *The Intelligence Gigantic* and *Liners of Time* (his first two novels), whilst the cream of his early short stories can be found in the two-volume set, *The Best of John Russell Fearn*. More recently, however, the Borgo Press has launched an ambitious program of reprinting all of Fearn's many detective novels (including new posthumous titles), together with new science fiction collections and novels.

This present novel, *Voice of the Conqueror*, was one of Fearn's later sf novels, first published (as *The Conqueror's Voice*) in 1954 in the prestigious Canadian magazine, the Toronto *Star Weekly*. It was then serialized as *Voice of the Conqueror* in the UK *British Science Fiction Magazine*, under Fearn's Vargo Statten pseudonym. It is a story which he clearly enjoyed writing, being partly based on personal experience.

Before the war, whilst Fearn was a full-time writer, his main hobby was the cinema. He was the proud owner of a 9.5 film projector, and used to throw shows to his friends at his home. The films were usually early old silent science fiction classics, such as *Metropolis*, *Caligari*, and *Girl in the Moon*. Fearn was to put his cinematic hobby to practical use in 1941, when Britain was in the grip of war.

At the outbreak of the war two years earlier, as a full-time writer over thirty (journalism being classed as a "Reserved Occupation"), Fearn was at first exempt from military service. But as the war continued, even journalists over thirty were called upon, and Fearn voluntarily took the medical test. However, he was adjudged as medically unsuitable. He was still obliged to undertake "essential war work," and so took a job in an aircraft factory. Fearn found the work arduous and crushing ("It damned near killed me," he later recalled) but fate soon intervened. What happened next was recorded in a letter Fearn sent to his Canadian pen friend Les Croutch, who published in it his fanzine *Light* in December 1941.

The previous summer, in a "dashing moment," Fearn had applied for a job as a cinema projectionist, but failed to get the job. "But my name was left on the books, and that was how my cinema manager friend (whom I've seen for years in the normal course of going to the movies) got onto it, him losing projectionists like wildfire where they are A1 medical (I'm C3, remember). I knew nothing about it beyond amateur work when I said I'd take it on, though I spun him a tale—but somehow I got through.... I got the breeze up the first time I opened out myself, but gradually I got a grip on things and now I feel quite at home."

I am indebted to Blackpool film and amateur dramatics historian Stephen Nuttall for providing further previously unrecorded fascinating information on Fearn's cinematic career. In 1998 Stephen published an interview he had conducted with Robert Simms, aged seventy-three, and living in retirement in a rural Fylde village, Little Eccleston.

In 1941, whilst Fearn was "winging" it as Chief Projectionist at Blackpool's down-market *Empire* cinema, the sixteen-year-old Simms was appointed as a trainee projectionist, or third operator, at the much more upmarket South Shore cinema, the *Tivoli*. Steve Nuttall's account continues:

"In 1943, Robert became a second operator and was then rapidly promoted again, within just one month, to the lofty position of chief operator. As he was little more than seventeen years old at the time, this made him not only the youngest chief in Lancashire, but also some months short of satisfying the legal minimum age requirement. To circumvent the law, the *Tivoli* employed Jack Russell Fearn, the locally-based science fiction writer, as projection room boss."

Bob Simms recalled his memories of the period to me in 2001. The situation could have been extremely awkward. Fearn completely lacked the technical experience to be Chief Projectionist at a larger cinema, and the young Simms actually knew far more about the job than he did. There could have been friction between them. But Bob found Fearn to be utterly disarming. He freely confessed his lack of knowledge, and was happy for the youngster to actually be in charge "behind the scenes." He was happy to assume the role of second projectionist. The two men became friends and got along "like a house on fire." Steve Nuttall again:

"Despite the fact that the precocious Robert could ably teach him everything he supposedly needed to know, the eccentric author, who was also a member of the Magic Circle, stayed quite aloof from the technical side of the job, preferring instead to regularly entertain the staff with his astonishing feats of prestidigitation."

Being an amateur magician was in fact another of Fearn's hobbies, and Bob recalls that he was an extremely good at it. His skill and good humour kept the cinema staff entertained during the long hours of what was something of an arduous job. As Nuttall explains:

"A typical day would begin at ten in the morning and finish around midnight. Moreover, if an air raid was in progress, the staff could sometimes be forced to spend an entire night in the building.... Robert recalls seeing low flying German aircraft passing regularly along the Fylde Coast to bomb Liverpool. As incredible as it may seem, Blackpool Tower was the safest site in the area due to the fact that the Luftwaffe used the famous landmark to gauge the precise co-ordinates for their deadly aerial assaults on Lancashire's principal seaport. From the vantage point of Fairhaven Lake, one could see the night sky all aglow as most of Merseyside tragically went up in flames. As one might expect, the task of fire watching was considered to be of primary importance; however, it does come as a surprise to learn that this was one of the duties that regularly befell Robert (as it did Fearn). Apparently, the job of cinema projectionist was deemed to be a "reserved occupation." After all, the cinema was no longer simply a venue for entertainment, but had a crucial role to play in the dissemination of information, including the showing of numerous training films for armed forces personnel and what some observers would label as propaganda movies."

Bob recalled to me that he discovered Fearn was a science fiction writer when he was briefly hospitalised. Fearn came to visit him, and loaned him a pile of his published stories in *Amazing Stories* and *Astounding Stories*, to help while away the hours. He quickly became a fan, and borrowed many more of Fearn's stories when he returned to work. He was fascinated to see Fearn scribbling away on notepads whilst the film reels were turning. During his time off, Fearn would then type up his notes and throughout the war, he continued to sell stories to the American pulp magazines. He also began to write more serious works, and Bob recalls that he was constantly revising his ms. of Blackpool life, *Little Winter*, the mainstream novel with which he hoped to break into higher literary markets. (Unfortunately the book was never published, and the ms. appears to have been destroyed.)

Projectionists were also responsible for operating

the background interval music, and Bob recalled to me that whenever Fearn was on duty and he spotted his beloved Mother in the audience, he would play her favourite piece of music, "Stardust" by Hoagy Carmichael. He remembers Fearn as an ingenious and fascinating character, and regretted losing contact when they went their separate ways.

In May 1945, following VE-Day, Fearn applied to the War Ministry for release from his job, in order to return to full-time writing. Permission was granted, and he gradually quit writing for the American pulp magazines as he became established in England as a novelist. Whereas his early magazine stories had been purely imaginative fiction, for his novels Fearn began to draw more upon his real-life experiences.

Fearn wrote several detective novels that centred around murders committed in a cinema, with the plots hinging on the technical side of film projection, and the cinema staff as leading characters (and murder suspects). They included *One Remained Seated* (1946) and an unpublished 1957 ms., *Many a Slip*. The latter novel was posthumously published as *Pattern of Murder* in 2005. Other "cinematic" sf novels included *The Grand Illusion* (1954) and *Voice of the Conqueror* (1954)

The name of the middle-aged "hero" of *Voice of the Conqueror* is 'Albert Simpkins,' known to his colleagues as "Old Simmy." Obviously, the surname is derived from Fearn's own work colleague Bob Simms, whom he knew as "Simmy." His actual character, however, is modeled on Fearn himself. Albert's fascination with science was clearly based on Fearn's own predilections.

The novel's extraordinary plot, telling how "old Simmy" actually succeeds in his idealistic dreams of reshaping the world, can be seen as amusing wish-fulfillment by the author. The scientific background to the novel is made up of several quite disparate elements. Some of them are extremely plausible and scientifically accurate (particularly on the cinematic side), and the concept of using an artificial satellite to broadcast worldwide radio messages is an inspired one. As everyone knows nowadays, the concept had, of course, first been visualized and invented by Arthur C. Clarke in his famous 1945 paper on "Extra-Terrestrial Relays." It is virtually certain that Fearn never saw this, or even knew of Clarke's idea, and if so he seems to have stumbled on the idea himself. Fearn's novel may well be one of the very first sustained fictional uses of the idea of broadcasting via an artificial satellite. (It was, of course, written some years before Sputnik and the actual advent of space travel.) One important difference was that Clarke visualized the satellite as *relaying* messages, rather than originating them.

Conversely, however, as was often the case with Fearn, some of the scientific background was highly implausible, and requires a willing suspension of disbelief. One of the enduring myths about early pulp science fiction was that stories supposedly abounded wherein a scientist built a spaceship in his own backyard! In actual fact, very few, if any, such stories exist! I have read as much early sf as most people, and I cannot remember reading a single example of this— except for Fearn's novel!

The author was of course well aware of the basic implausibility of this, and so, in the style of the skilled science fictionist, he tries to make it plausible. In my view, he succeeds in doing so by sheer storytelling skill, and in his sympathetic portrayal of the altruistic Albert Simpkins, he obviously wrote from his own personal beliefs. This gives the story a definite believ-ability, and adds to its appeal.

CHAPTER ONE

Because Albert Simpkins looked a fool, everybody believed he was one. Yes, everybody. The only one who had known he was *not* a fool was dead, and that had been his mother. Being a quite normal woman, she knew she had not given to the world a genius, but on the other hand she had not produced a fool either. It was just a case of looks being deceptive.

Albert Simpkins was forty-five, but prematurely thinning hair made him look ten years older. He held the not too lofty position of chief projectionist in a local cinema, a position to which he clung with all his might because here, in his own little domain, he was absolute boss. At least he had reached the top as far as buildings were concerned. Here he had the chance to exercise traits of character that were normally crushed—and the boy and youth who worked with him as assistants were fairly obedient, mainly because they rather liked "Old Simmy."

It was at home where Albert Simpkins received the biggest blows. At twenty-five he had married Emily Dawson. At that time she had been a fetching cashier with curly blonde hair and an infectious smile. Albert had then been a second projectionist, and they had walked home together. Inevitably, they had seen the future as all sunbeams, romance, and progress—and now, twenty years later, in the present-day hurrying scientific world, they found themselves very much wearied with each other, just about able to get along, and saddled with the responsibility of three daughters and a son. Yes, Albert Simpkins had a lot on his mind and little in his pocket.

"It wouldn't be so bad, Emily," he said one evening, when he had returned from his usual night's work at the Premier Cinema, "if Bob could be made to cough up what rightly belongs to me. We'd have plenty then."

"Dreams!" Emily sighed. "Like everything else you indulge in! Empty, silly dreams! Bob will never give you anything, and you know it!"

Albert was silent, realising that Emily was probably right. Bob Simpkins was Albert's elder brother, possessed of all the terrific self-assurance that Albert completely lacked. He was a big man in the grocery distribution business somewhere in North London, and spent his time making his money, and his spare moments sneering at failures. By some kind of legal know-how that Albert had never been able to fathom, his brother had claimed all the money left in Mrs. Simpkins' will. It had been a fair sum, for Mrs. Simpkins had had plenty at her death. The net result was that the roaring, domineering Bob had got the lot and—as usual—Albert had got nothing. Emily knew the facts, and so did the children. Because of them

Albert was considered to be an even bigger fool than his appearance suggested.

"No," Emily decided, hauling her fat back as she rolled in her chair at the supper table, "Bob will never give you a thing—unless it's a slap on the back that will knock you silly. Sillier, that is, than you are already."

Albert looked at her and did not like what he saw. In twenty years Emily had become gray-haired, and so fat it was difficult to tell where her head ended and her shoulders began. Of course her eyes were still blue, but this was all that remained of the once-laughing girl who had waved a torch so adroitly for the latecomers at the Premier Cinema.

As for Albert, he was pinched and pale. His lack of color was not so much due to ill health as to the constant inhalation of carbon fumes from the projectors. Twenty years of breathing in poison had left their mark. He looked unhappy and somewhat vacant, though actually his uncomprehending gaze was born of the fact that lie was always dreaming—dreaming of that which he had not got. Money, fame, fortune, all the world at his feet. Yet—and here was the unusual thing—Albert believed he could have all these things if he could only pin together several really bright ideas that for years had been chasing around in his mind in dissociated form. It was just a matter of linking them up, and some day he would.

"Where are the kids?" he asked presently, *apropos* of nothing, and Emily yawned.

"Dick and Betty are in bed. Ethel's not got back yet

from night school, and Vera's been out since seven with young Hal Morrison. They're in a dancing competition or something."

"Mmmm." Albert finished drinking his tea. "Be a help if Hal would take Vera off our hands. One less to bother about."

"Wouldn't make any difference. Ethel makes enough to keep herself. If she went, we'd still be where we are now—on the edge of the rocks."

Albert muttered something to himself and got to his feet. He wandered about the untidy little kitchen for a moment or two, then selected one of the dozens of scientific magazines lying in a haphazard pile in a corner and sat in the worn armchair to read. Emily's blue eyes followed his movements and her cushiony lips compressed.

"*That's* what I complain about with you, Albert. When you haven't your job to do, you waste your time instead of improving it! Most men, when the day's work is done, spend their time thinking up ways to get more money and improve the lot of themselves and their families. But not you! Oh, no! You have to read all this scientific trash—day in, night out. Every spare moment! What good does it do you?"

Albert turned the worn magazine pages slowly but did not look up. "It never hurts to improve the mind, Emmy. I don't get much chance to relax, remember. Matinees and evening shows swallow up a lot of time, and on my day off, I've things to do—tidying the garden, titivating the house, and so on. 'Sides, I like reading about scientific things when we live in a scientific age. Won't be long now the way rocketry is progressing before travel into space becomes an everyday thing."

"I'm not interested in reaching the moon! I'm only interested that you should better things. You've got to forty-five and haven't done it yet. Doesn't leave much time, you know. Dreams! Always dreams!"

"Uh-huh," Albert sighed. "Pretty well all I have left these days, Emmy.... Yet, you know," he continued, his eyes brightening a little, "there's one dream which I believe I shall one day make come true. And if I do I'll be—"

"Oh, such rubbish!" Emily surged to her feet, disgusted, her immense bosom flopping. "It's a waste of time talking to you. Here, give me a hand with these crocks and leave that scientific rubbish until later. It'll keep."

Uncomplaining, Albert tossed the magazine down upon its battered companions and struggled out of the armchair. Thereafter, in pensive silence, he helped his ample spouse with the washing-up, and such was the scientific slant in his mentality he actually seemed to find something intriguing in the way the soap-suds exploded on her fleshy forearms as she savagely swabbed the plates and cups.

"If you'd get an automatic washer instead of dreaming, we'd be better off!" she commented acidly. "I'm getting past doing all the washing, cleaning, pot washing, ironing, and chores *ad infinitum.* Sometimes

I wonder why I ever quit working as a cashier. Might even go back to it. They take 'em at forty-five even now. Some cinemas prefer them. You're not prone to goings-on in the dark when you're forty-five."

"Know something, Emmy? Those suds explode on your skin because of the air pressure inside being greater than that outside. A simple scientific fact, and yet it has interest."

"Has it?" Emily stared at her wet forearms. "What on earth are you talking about?"

"Just thinking out loud. The idea I have chasing around in my mind hasn't anything to do with soap-suds, but the basic principle is just as simple."

This time Emily did not say anything. She was accustomed to Albert talking in this vague fashion, and since none of his theories seemed to crystallize into anything, she considered them beneath her notice.

"I suppose," she resumed presently, as the washing-up came to an end, "that you propose to end your days at the Premier, if the management tolerate you that long?"

"Maybe. Maybe not. Depends how much I learn. It can be quite interesting in a projection room, Emmy. The scientific side of it fascinates me, particularly the interpretation of sound by light through the transparent track on the side of the film. Then again, the three-dimensional illusion is one of the big—"

"You missed this cup and saucer," Emily interrupted, and brought the conversation to a close.

And it remained at a close until bedtime. Ethel

and Vera came home in the interval, but had little to say to their father as once more he browsed through his scientific magazine and took not the least notice of their teenage vaporings. It was not that he had no interest in his daughters—he was merely dominated by the theories that wove constantly through his mind.

"The main thing wrong with this world, Emmy," he said, when he and his wife had at last retired, "is that there's too much selfishness. Too much greed. Take Bob, for example. If he were not so greedy he—"

"He knows how to take care of himself anyway, and that's more than you can do!"

The blow went fully home, and Albert subsided, but long after his wife had fallen asleep he still remained awake, staring at the ceiling vaguely patterned from the street light outside the house. It was in the quiet of the night, when he lay like this, no longer in fear of derision or interruption, that his thoughts had a chance to link up all the scattered theories he had been gathering for so long a time. And he felt that if only he could perhaps.... Then he was asleep, to awaken again to the drabness of the autumn morning.

So to the usual routine—the hurried breakfast, then out to the Premier Cinema with its dank morning coldness and smell of amyl-acetate. His two assistants were already at work re-spooling film from the previous night's performance. They greeted Albert perfunctorily as he arrived, but he took little notice of them. Instead he set to work with a newly purchased writing-pad and left the bulk of the projection room cleaning routine to the two boys. What he was doing he would not say, but from what the boys could see he appeared to be immersed in mathematics.

During the matinee that day he had to give his attention whether he wanted to or not, and again at the evening performance. But when the evening show was over, he made no attempt—as he usually did—to don his hat and overcoat. Instead he lingered around the winding-room with its smell of dead carbon fumes.

"Not coming, Simmy?" asked the youth who was second projectionist.

"Later." Albert's look was faraway. "I want to check the new program which came in this morning. We're showing it the day after tomorrow, and I can't entirely trust it to you lads."

"Oh!" The boys glanced at one another, puzzled. This was the first time Albert had ever doubted their proficiency.

"Not that I'm thinking you don't know your jobs," Albert amended, "but we're having the mayor or some local bigwig coming on Saturday night, and any mistakes would be fatal. See you in the morning."

"Okay, Simmy."

"Night, Simmy."

To the manager Albert gave the same story, but since Albert had been in the cinema for twenty years there seemed no reason to question his purpose. In any case he had his own key. So Albert was finally left to his own devices.

It was well after half-past one in the small hours when

at last he left the cinema and went home through the silent streets. He knew Emily would not be concerned by his non-arrival home, for very frequently he ran a midnight matinee to correct some imperfection in a program to be shown the following day. Nor was his guess wrong. Emily was snoring soundly when at last, after a cold supper, he got to bed—and the next morning did not even trouble to ask what had delayed him.

But even Emily began to wonder a little when Albert did not come home until the small hours for a whole fortnight. She knew midnight matinees could not explain *this*, and her mind began to stray towards the possibility of a meek-and-mild Albert leading a double life.

Emily was not the only one who wondered. The manager of the cinema wondered too, and since he was in command he wasted no time in getting at the truth. So, after his fortnight of mysterious nocturnal activity Albert found himself summoned to the manager's office.

"Just checking up on something, Albert." The manager was breezily friendly as usual. "What's the idea of staying behind until the small hours every night for the last two weeks? Can't be program trouble, surely?"

Albert hesitated, clearly a little startled. "Who says I've stayed behind?"

"Nobody. It just happens that the policeman on the beat around this cinema calls back his headquarters from the police phone on the corner around one-thirty, and each night he has noticed a figure answering your description leaving the cinema. He reported it to me, wondering if all was well. Be you, of course?"

"Yes," Albert agreed absently. "Yes, it was."

"Well? Why do you do it? Don't love the place *that* much after twenty years, surely?"

"No. As a matter of fact I've been checking over the projectors. They need a routine once-over now and again."

"Why? We have a service engineer for that!" Suspicion was slowly forming on the manager's face, and his smile had gone.

Albert was silent; then suddenly he seemed to come to a decision. "I spent the time reading," he said quickly. "It was the only way in which I could read in peace. At home I have a somewhat talkative wife and four children, and when a man wants to study things out he—"

"Look, Albert!" The manager's voice was curt. "I'm not interested in your domestic life, but I *am* interested in the electricity bill for this cinema, and so are the owners to whom I'm responsible. You've no right to burn up light in the projection room for the purpose of reading until the small hours of the morning. See it doesn't happen again, and we'll say no more about it."

"Well—all right," Albert muttered, and with that took his departure.

But the odd thing was that he did not keep his word. That night he stayed again until the small hours—indeed, until five in the morning, having nailed a cardboard poster of a famous film star over the winding-room window to prevent the light being seen from outside. Then towards dawn, red-eyed and weary, he crawled home for a few hours' sleep, and at breakfast found Emily staring at him with naked questions sparking in her eyes.

"You're up to something!" she declared, handing across the grilled bacon.

"Oh, let me alone," Albert growled, leaden from continuous night work and—had anybody else known it—intensely close and concentrated work.

"I *won't* let you alone! For over a fortnight you've never come home until early morning. This time it was half-past five! I know because I was awake."

"Turned into a burglar, pop?" asked the youngest daughter, and then shrieked with merriment.

"You've got to be tough to burgle," Ethel commented, shaking her head. "Doesn't fit dad at all!"

Albert got to his feet abruptly, his face flushed and his eyes hard. For an instant it looked as if he were going to blow his whole family wide open for the first time in his life; then he thought better of it, and without a word left the room and slammed the door.

Ten minutes later he entered the cinema, nodded moodily to the cleaner-*cum*-commissionaire, and then found the manager right in front of him. The manager's face was grim and unsmiling as he nodded towards his office.

"Sorry, Albert," he said quietly, following Albert in and closing the door. "The owners don't like the way you've been behaving. I had to report your late hours to them to explain the use of extra electricity, and I told them you wouldn't do it again. But you did, and left later—or earlier—than ever! Five o'clock! One of the owners had a man posted to watch...."

Albert was silent.

"It's a pity," the manager said, sighing. "After twenty years of good service. You've got to go, though. Don't blame me—I'm only doing as I'm told. Here are your insurance cards."

Albert took them and smiled wryly. "Fired, you mean?"

"As from now. Wages up to date and a week ahead. Why the devil you were such a chump I'll never understand."

"No, you'll never understand," Albert admitted vaguely, pushing the cards in his pocket. "Doesn't matter much, anyway. I've finished what I had to do, which was why I stayed extra late last night."

"Your reading, you mean?"

"Uh-huh; might as well call it that. Anyway, don't worry over me. Twenty years in one place is too long anyhow. Wish the staff the best of luck for me, will you?'

The manager nodded slowly, surprise obvious on his round face. He watched Albert leave the office, entirely preoccupied, and the door closed. Still in the same lost frame of mind Albert returned home—and Emily gazed at him as though he were a visitor from Mars.

"You! At this hour! What's the matter? Feeling ill?"

"No; quite well. Better than I've felt for twenty years. Did you never accomplish something, Emmy, just in time before the fall of the axe?"

"Eh?"

Albert sighed and relaxed in the armchair. "Never mind. You wouldn't understand."

"I *can* understand that you're at home when you ought to be at work. What's *wrong*?"

"I got fired. Working too late and burning too much light. Doesn't matter. The firm can afford it, and I can't. Besides, I had everything I needed there, and I haven't here."

"Fired, did you say?" Emily gave a start. "Great heavens, you've lost your job after twenty years? What did you *do*?"

"I just told you. But don't let it worry you. I'll take a day or two off and then get another job of a totally different type. Something scientific after my own heart."

Emily looked as though she would open the floodgates, but she did not. She knew, too, that she ought to feel fearful for the future, but here again her emotions did not register that way. Albert was looking mysteriously confident and certainly not like a man who has lost a job and has no other in sight.

It did indeed take him a fortnight to discover a fresh situation—a lowly one indeed—as a cleaner in a laboratory devoted to electronics. Emily could not appreciate that it was the electronics that appealed to Albert, not the humdrum procedure of mopping floors and dusting endless shelves.

The laboratory was one of fifty scattered up and down Britain under the new Science and Electronics legislation, by which all scientists of all European countries were teamed together to pool their knowledge. Every branch of science was included under the new law, but chiefly experimental work in electronics, guided missiles, and tests of interplanetary space were being carried out—this latter by means of high altitude rockets loaded with instruments.

CHAPTER TWO

Into this web-work of science, therefore, came Albert—quiet, mysteriously confident about something, offering himself to No. 9 Laboratory in North London as a cleaner.

"Done laboratory work before?" questioned the sharp-eyed doyen who controlled the establishment.

"No, sir." Albert gave a meek smile. "I hardly see that cleaning a laboratory can be very different from cleaning anywhere else. It's simply the process of removing dirt."

"It is more than that, Simpkins. You may get mixed up with radioactive isotopes and all manner of things. Part of the time you may even have to wear protective suiting. I'm warning you in advance in case the job doesn't appeal."

"It appeals immensely, sir. I feel at home amongst scientific apparatus. I've studied science as a hobby all my life."

"I see." The doyen studied the filing system. "Formerly a chief projectionist, eh? Mmmm, scientific after a fashion. Integrity beyond question. Very well, Simpkins, the job is yours at the salary quoted in the advertisement. You are prepared to sign a bond of fidelity that no word shall ever escape you as to any scientific experiment which you may witness whilst employed here?"

"Quite prepared, sir."

"Right!" And upon appending his signature, Albert became one of the staff. His salary was far below that which he had formerly earned, but he was entirely happy. Emily, on the other hand, was exactly the opposite, and never forgot to upbraid him every time he returned from his slogging and cleaning.

"I can't imagine what you're thinking of!" she declared flatly one evening when she and Albert were alone. "You have a profession in your hands as a projectionist—and in the present cinema boom there's plenty need of them—and yet you're content to clean floors!"

"Not by any means, Emmy. I'm learning a lot. All about altitude rockets, supersonics, electronics, and a host of scientific accomplishments. Besides, I'm friendly with several of the senior scientists who'll always talk to anybody interested in science, even if he is only a cleaner—and they are giving me valuable information."

"What about, for heaven's sake?"

"About those theories I've been tossing round in my mind for so many years. I'm tying them up now, one by one, and in the finish I'll have one grand, practical plan. Then things will really happen."

"What things?" Emily was relentless.

Albert gazed into the fire. "Emmy, I once said that all

the unhappiness in the world is caused by selfishness and greed. Suppose something happened to change all that? Suppose people everywhere did the right thing because they just couldn't do anything else?"

"Ridiculous! More of your crazy dreaming, Albert!"

"No." Albert shook his head slowly, his eyes having a light in them that Emily had never seen before. "No, Emmy, it isn't crazy. It's practical. Everything I am doing is with a fixed purpose. Just leave me alone and wait. A day will come when we'll not only have all the money we need, but all the happiness as well.... It isn't natural that living, thinking beings should be anything else *but* happy. That's part of my philosophy."

"Then it's out of joint! Everybody's unhappy about something. I defy you to find a really contented person on the face of the earth!"

"At the moment you're right. But later...." Albert, however, had drifted off into speculations, and Emily could not get any further explanations from him. Finally she gave it up, and Albert returned to his inevitable magazine.

So, for many weeks, matters pursued an apparently humdrum course. Albert came and went at his cleaning job, saying little to Emily because she had not the kind of mind to understand him. The one thing she *could* understand, however, was that Albert began to bring home odd pieces of equipment concealed in his overalls, and by degrees they began to occupy quite a fair space in the outhouse—normally used for bicycles and lawn-mower.

"Are you sure," Emily asked uneasily, "that you're doing right in bringing home stuff like this?"

"Quite sure. It's mainly throw-out stuff, and I've asked permission to keep some of it. As a cleaner I'm well in touch with the laboratory junk."

"Junk, yes, but the stuff I've seen looks like perfectly good electrical equipment and worth a fair sum of money."

"It would be if it were not defective. Everything's all right, Emmy, believe me. In any case, you can't get in or out of a Government laboratory without the most rigid overhaul. Detector beams and heaven knows what go to work on you as you enter and leave the building, just so as to be sure you're not carrying anything you shouldn't."

Emily nodded even though she found it hard to believe. But Albert was telling the truth. The stuff he had appropriated was quite valueless to the laboratory, where precision to the *nth* degree was required, and he had been given permission to take some of the stuff away—supposedly to form the basis of a color television receiver. Only Albert had far higher dreams than this!

He had very little spare time—Emily saw to that—but whenever he could seize a few moments, he tinkered away in the outhouse with his queer gadgets, coils of wire, and linked-up batteries. Where apparatus was defective he rectified it, and quite skilfully too. Accordingly, by degrees, there began to appear something that looked like a cross between a radio set and a tape-recorder.

The youngsters wanted to know what it was all about, and had to be satisfied with a vague explanation about a 3-D color televisor. Emily wanted to know everything too, and learned precisely nothing. Nor could she or the children examine the mystery apparatus in their spare time because Albert bought an old but sturdy safe of considerable dimensions and kept the apparatus locked away in it whenever he was absent from home.

Apparently the "Televisor" was not the limit of his ambition, however, for presently he began to construct another kind of instrument. It looked like a clock and was superbly designed. Even Emily had to admit that. Nobody would ever have guessed that Albert was the veriest amateur. But then, he had the constructional pages of his science magazine to help him.

By the spring his "clock" was complete, and by now it formed the apparent nucleus of another piece of equipment, in the center of which the "clock" was embedded. There were tubes in this external equipment—tubes, wires, small transformers, and a host of other things utterly baffling to anybody except Albert, or maybe a trained scientist.

Albert was sensible enough, however, to realize that you cannot fool all the people all the time. So, of his own free will he suddenly condescended to explain to the family what he was driving at, and he chose a warm evening in spring when Emily, Ethel, Dick, Betty, and Vera were all at home, an event of unusual rarity.

"Things," Albert said, with an air of tremendous

assurance, "are very shortly going to happen! Because you'll be involved in these things as much as anybody else, you might as well have advance warning. I've been working on a master-plan, and it's about complete."

"Taken a long time," Emily commented, darning a sock with vicious needle thrusts.

"All scientific accomplishments take a long time; only to be expected. However, to come to the point, I've been devising a way of making myself master of the world without afterwards cashing-in on the undoubted opportunities afforded by such a lofty position."

"Eh?" Emily sat up and stared, her darning forgotten. As for the younger ones, they simply regarded their father as though he had gone completely crazy.

"Master of the world," Albert repeated, sitting back in the worn armchair and wagging his head to himself. "And the best of it is, nobody will know it's me. It will sound as though some all-powerful visitor from outer space is giving the orders. And, what is more, getting them obeyed! Think how much good that will do in the world."

"Why will it?" Emily asked stupidly. "And who's going to obey *you*, anyhow?"

"Everybody who hears the voice. The Conqueror's Voice! How's that sound?"

"It sounds all right, but coming from you it's a farce! The last thing I can picture is you as a conqueror!"

"I know. Practically everybody who knows me feels the same way." Albert clenched his bony fists and his eyes were gleaming. "That's what has been wrong all through my life. I've been taken for a meek, down-trodden fool, which is one reason why I've turned my scientific talent to righting the wrong that has been done me. From here on I intend to sit back and watch anybody do exactly as I say!"

Vera, the eldest child, gave a rather sardonic laugh. "Even if that could happen, dad—which it obviously can't—you'd very soon find yourself run in if you tried it. It'd be a short cut to the booby-hatch. Delusions of grandeur, or something."

Albert looked at her. "You listen to me, my girl. You've heard of a perfect crime, haven't you? The kind of crime so brilliantly executed that nobody can tell how it was done?"

"Of course I have!"

"Well, this is similar. Only instead of being a crime, it's a blessing, or intended to be. Nobody will ever be able to prove who's back of it, and unless my calculations are utterly wrong, everybody will think an outer-space visitor is the culprit. Certainly nobody will suspect Albert Simpkins."

Ethel tittered, and Vera gave her mother an anxious glance. "Mum, I don't think dad's very well. He can't be! He talks of being master of the world, yet he can't even make his own family obey him."

"Under the old order I couldn't, certainly," Albert admitted, "but I've found a different way of controlling things. Just let me explain further."

"By all means!" Emily exclaimed, still looking stunned. Getting quickly to his feet, Albert left the room, and he could well imagine the kind of conversation that was taking place during his absence. When he returned, he found each member of the family quiet, but studying him in suspicious wonder. The wonder deepened as he set upon the table his strange clock device with its outer mechanism of tubes, minute transformers, and intricate wiring.

"This thing operates over a distance of twenty feet," he explained, plugging it into the nearby power point. "It will also operate from batteries. Now, Vera, my smart young lady, let's see what sort of a brain you've got."

"What!" Vera jumped up in alarm, her eyes wide in obvious fright. "Don't you dare come near me with that thing, dad!"

"I've no need to. Your brain has already given its emanation. Want to see for yourself?"

Vera hesitated, noting that her father had been operating both a graded wheel and a kind of rheostat knob, meanwhile watching the queer behavior of the central needle on the "clock."

"Don't you go near it!" Emily warned—but Vera was young and therefore curious. She moved forward and peered at the instrument cautiously. The "clock" needle was pointing, she observed, to number 9865 amongst the scale readings, which went up to 10,000. The scale was plainly a professional job and the work of precision engineers, but the omission of two numbers had led the government to throw the gadget out—with a government's usual prodigal extravagance—which had become Albert's gain.

"This," Albert explained, as Vera stood beside him and the rest of the family now moved up in curiosity, "is what I call a brain-frequency detector. In case you don't know it, Vera—as you hardly can—your brain is constantly giving forth electric waves."

"Yes?" Vera looked very dumb, like her mother. "Honest?"

"Not just your brain either, but everybody's—a fact which I learned from my science magazines. What is more, just as Mother Nature never produces two sets of identical fingerprints, she also never produces two sets of identical brain frequencies. Of all the countless millions of souls there are in the world, every one has a different frequency."

"Then why," Vera asked, who was a cashier and proud of her mathematics, "does your dial only register up to ten thousand?"

"For ten thousand read a hundred million," her father replied. "I'm making do with this throw-out dial and improvising the figures as need be. Your brain frequency isn't nine eight six five, but nearer the hundred million mark, and these myriad hair-line divisions make up the intermediates. See?"

"No!" Emily declared flatly. "And I think it's a lot of rot!"

"This clock thing," Albert continued, undisturbed, "is the main detector needle. If I am within twenty feet of any living being and depress the control button here, the frequency of that person's brain is immediately registered. From this instrument there goes forth an invisible beam direct to the person concerned—which insulates other people who might be present from also registering—and back along the beam on the principle of a radar echo comes the brain frequency. It is then registered in stopwatch fashion on this dial. So far, so good."

"More than good," Vera corrected, wondering. "It's mighty near a miracle."

"Having once found a brain frequency, I know exactly how to control that frequency."

Silence. The younger members of the family wandered away, no longer interested. Vera and her mother remained, just to see how far this business was going to develop.

"It is an elementary fact," Albert explained, "that when you have the given electrical frequency of any emanation, you can control it by the use of another frequency which is in exact 'sympathy.' That, basically, is the principle of remote control of airplanes, guided missiles, and so forth. In this case, though, I'm dealing with a more rarefied product—the emanation of thought waves."

"You mean you can tell what people are thinking?" Emily asked, with sudden brightness, but Albert shook his head.

"No, dear, that's telepathy. This is control. Hypnotism, if you like, mechanically applied instead of by the usual method. It amounts to this: a certain frequency is given off by the brain; an identical frequency is used to control it. It also follows that if thought waves can travel back along the original detector beam, other thought waves can travel *forward* along the control beam. And since the power of the control beam will be many times stronger than that of the detector, the outcome is obvious. Absolute mental control of the subject."

"Sounds diabolical," Vera said, pondering. "Like Svengali and that wench who sang for him. Trilby, wasn't it?"

"This is scientific," Albert said simply. "And so easy. I can command obedience as the mind behind the control beam. For instance, Vera, if I tuned in to your frequency, this is what would happen—"

Vera had not the least idea what did happen, but the rest of the family had. They watched her go to the armchair and, heavy though it was, she raised it with ease and put it on the broad table. Not satisfied with this, she made a leap that would have done credit to a circus acrobat, vaulting straight from the floor into the armchair seat. There she remained, singing in a clear soprano voice the immortal aria, "One Fine Day."

"See what I mean?" Albert asked dryly, and switched off.

There was now a stunned and overpowering quietness. Emily looked as though her eyes had become twice as large as normal. Ethel, Betty, and Dick remained in a corner, muttering among themselves. Up in the armchair Vera stirred and looked about her. Then she started.

"In heavens' name, how did I get up here?"

"You got there because I commanded it," her father replied, holding up his hand to help her descend. "I have satisfied myself on three things. One, the control beam produces absolute mastery of the subject; two, the subject can be made to do things beyond the normal; and three, an ability in a certain direction can be instantly developed without the need of wearisome training. That satisfies the point that the body doesn't matter. It's the *mind* that does the work. Believe a thing sufficiently and nothing can stand in your way, and least of all the body. You, Vera, are not a strongwoman of the circus variety, yet you tossed that armchair about with perfect ease. You're not a professional athlete either, yet you took a jump worthy of any sportswoman. Finally, you are not a singer, yet you sang an aria with all the clarity of a prima Donna."

"*I* did?" Vera jabbed a finger towards herself and blinked. "But—but I don't remember it!"

"How could you? My mind, amplified by this apparatus, carried the commands. The outflowing beam being so powerful, your own individual will foundered beneath it.... Now you see what I mean when I say I can have the world at my feet! Not a living soul can stand against this!"

If Albert expected intelligent reaction he was disappointed, for the whole business was too utterly overpowering. He gave a rather grave smile.

"You should consider yourselves privileged in that you have had this little demonstration," he said. "There is a great deal more than this, though, far too complicated for me to waste my time telling you. You'll see just how far-reaching this system can be as time goes on. Now perhaps you understand why I say that henceforth I shall be the master, not only of and in everyday affairs, but also in my own house?"

"But—but you can't mean that you intend to use that terrible thing on us!" Emily cried, horrified.

"That is up to you. If you desist from your constant ridicule—and that applies to all of you—and treat me with the respect to which I'm entitled as the head of the household, then all will be well. If you do not—well, I have all your frequency numbers, which each one of you has unwittingly given me when prowling around my private outhouse, and to each number there is the control counterpart. It's up to you," Albert finished, laying a hand on the instrument, and his smile was full of significance.

CHAPTER THREE

Awe-stricken by the manner in which the normally strong-willed, self-opinionated Vera had been compelled to act contrary to her inclinations, Albert's annoying family took the lesson to heart and thereafter said nothing derogatory about him. This was no more than he expected. Be it said to his credit that it was not that he wished to browbeat his wife and children—he simply pined for acknowledgement of the scientific genius that was unquestionably his. He felt that scientific historians would probably bracket his name with that of Edison, Marconi, and Baird.

Meanwhile, he formulated further plans. He had not spoken idly when he had said he meant to be master of the world, just for the fun of it, without ever using the vast power such a position would carry with it.

Continuing his menial cleaning job at No. 9 Laboratory, he spent a great deal of time keeping his eyes and ears open. He talked with eminent scientists and bright-eyed young theorists: he even tackled an intricate problem or two with the dean of the establishment. He gained permission to spend three evenings a week watching a special staff of scientists at work on guided missiles, designed for the remote-control exploration of outer space. He learned, and learned, and learned, but always remained strictly within the boundaries laid down for secrecy.

Then one evening, having forewarned his wife, he made a trip to north London where lay the large, comfortable home of his brother Bob. He did not actually call upon him, however. Instead, he went into the park near his brother's home and there, on the form on which he sat, he deposited the heavy box of apparatus that he had brought with him, carrying it mainly by the shoulder strap. It had been a bit of a risk hauling the box around. He had brought it from home during the morning, hidden it in a ditch near the laboratory grounds whilst he had worked, and picked it up again on departure. To his heartfelt relief, nobody had chanced upon it.

Now he sat in the mellow glow of the spring evening, smiling serenely to himself, and carefully lifting the lid of the apparatus. The self-contained batteries operated instantly as he moved the switch, and a little fiddling with the directional knobs very soon enabled him to direct an "echo" beam at his brother's home, visible just beyond the recreation ground.

Albert knew exactly what he was doing. His brother had written to say that he was a "grass widower" whilst the wife and kids were on holiday. He had also said he was coming home every afternoon so he could attend to much private business in peace. If the beam reacted, he would be the only person on whom it could have impinged, and—

It *did* react, almost immediately. Without haste Albert studied the reading-number, and then glanced about him. There was nobody important in sight. The nearest sign of life lay in a party of children gambolling in the grass, and they were not in the least interested in Albert and his mystery box.

He switched into "Control," and then opened the circuit that activated the magnetic plates for receiving his own outflowing thought waves. He spent no more than three minutes concentrating; then he quietly packed the instrument up again and went on his way, looking curiously like some itinerant musician without a monkey.

He reached home an hour and a half late to find his tea—a mess of fried fish, which he thoroughly detested—was being kept warm for him. Emily did not say anything much. Ever since the night of Vera's transient "conversion" she had been particularly guarded, but that she was curious was obvious.

"I think," Albert said, gratifying her when he had freshened up, "that we shall have a visit from Bob this evening."

"Lord!" Emily made a wry face.

"In fact I'm *sure*," Albert confirmed. "Since his visit will benefit us considerably, we must do our best to treat him as hospitably as possible."

"He's your brother and you know how difficult he is. All swank, and brag, and publicity—"

"I know. Nevertheless, it has to be endured."

Emily poured out some tea and then frowned. "What makes you so sure he's coming? Has he said so? I thought his letter said he was staying at home to—"

"He is coming," Albert interposed calmly, "because I have ordered him to do so."

"You don't mean—that *machine*?"

"Yes."

Emily moved uncomfortably and handed across the tea.

"You shouldn't do such things, Albert. It isn't natural! It's against all the laws of—of.... Anyway, it's wrong."

"Not at all! It's scientific. Besides, I need a great deal of money, and Bob is the one to get it for me."

"I don't see the point of that. You've got that horrible Compulsion Machine of yours. Why don't you walk into a bank and use it?"

Albert sighed. "How little you understand of the principle I'm trying to live up to. I am perfectly aware that I could walk into a bank and have as much money as necessary given to me by a hypnotized staff. I am also aware that I could force any man or woman on this earth to degrade him or herself before all the world— only I'm not that kind of man. Remember the old saying—'As you are powerful, be merciful.' I feel—"

"Oh, be hanged to proverbs, Albert! Why use Bob for money when you have the chance of demanding it elsewhere?"

"Because I want the money as honestly and unostentatiously as possible. If I did get it from a bank by dishonest means, I'd very soon be caught out. Can't you see that I'm trying to use my discovery of remote-control compulsion to an entirely good end? I'm a world reformer of the most novel, orthodox kind. But greatest of all is the thought of the kick I shall get out of forcing certain people to do just as they're told. The days of Albert Simpkins, prize fool, are over."

Emily did not say anything. She drank some dregs of cool tea unintentionally and made a wry face.

"Where are the youngsters?" Albert asked presently.

"Vera and Ethel are playing tennis. Dick and Betty are in the park somewhere. Do them good on a nice evening like this. Does it matter?"

"No. I just prefer to keep them out of the way when Bob's here. They might talk too much, recalling Vera's unrehearsed demonstration, for instance. You'll keep them quiet, Emmy?"

"If you say so."

With which Albert was satisfied. He finished his tea leisurely, spent a while working out some problem for himself whilst Emily cleared the tea things and dusted the room—then promptly at eight o'clock the doorbell rang.

"I'll deal with it," Albert said, rising. "You keep a firm hand on the kids."

He left the kitchen and passed through the hall to the front door. Bob was there—a fat and loud-voiced edition of Albert himself. Out shot his red paw.

"Well, if it isn't the old 'Has Been' himself! How's tricks? Bet you didn't expect me, eh?"

"Matter of fact, I had a kind of intuition," Albert

replied vaguely. "Come in. Glad to see you."

"Glad? Glad! Hell, that's a new one! How're Emmy and the offspring?"

"Well enough, thanks." Albert followed his brother into the drawing room and closed the door. Bob threw himself into the nearest armchair and gave a direct glance from his bloodshot eyes.

"Look, Al. I've been doing a lot of thinking lately. You won't know what that means the way you mope around—but I did get around to thinking that maybe I've been a bit tough with you."

Albert sat down and held out a cigarette packet. "Tough? In what way?"

"Well, over mother's will, for instance. I held out on you regarding it. Trickery, you know! Don't know why I should be such a damned fool as to come and admit it, but there it is. Generous at heart! That's me."

"I know you tricked me, but I could never quite see how."

"Lot of things you don't see, Al. That's your trouble. It was legal twisting, and I felt kind of proud of it at the time. But lately, having had time to think with the wife out of the way, I came to realizing that you're a pretty downtrodden blighter and can't have much of the ready to play with. So—" Bob spread his hands. "I've decided to become generous."

"To what extent?"

"Well, by the terms of mother's will half of her money is due to you. I needed that extra fifty percent pretty badly at the time of the will being proved, which is why I—er—"

"Wangled things?" Albert suggested calmly, and Bob looked under his eyes.

"Yes. I can un-wangle them just as easily without causing any trouble. I'm sort of throwing myself on your mercy. If you want an exposure instead, you won't have a leg to stand on, because there is no witness to what we are discussing now."

Albert shrugged. "You're my brother, after all, and blood's thicker than water. You get that money due to me sorted, and I'll keep perfectly quiet. Glad you decided to act honestly. It pays in the long run."

Bob got to his feet—a most uneasy-looking, deflated Bob. There was too a peculiarly dazed look in his eyes, which only Albert could have explained.

"Anything wrong?" Albert asked, after a moment.

"Not exactly wrong. I just feel funny somehow. Felt it all evening. Maybe blood pressure catching up on me—"

"Stay and have a drink? Can't make it stronger than tea or coffee, I'm afraid."

"Never mind. It'd mean meeting Emily, and I know she doesn't like me. Can't understand why you ever married that girl."

"Lots of things about me you don't understand, Bob."

Bob gave a puzzled look and then turned to the door. A few moments later he had departed, and Albert wandered back pensively into the kitchen. He found Emily there, lolling in the armchair, her ample arms locked beneath her flopping bosom. At the table Betty was catching up on belated homework, whilst young Dick was busy binding a split cricket bat. Of the elder girls there was no sign, therefore Albert felt he could talk freely.

"We've come into a fortune, Emmy," he said simply, but Emily remained unmoved.

"Because Bob says so? When I start to believe him, Albert, the heavens will fall."

"This is different. He doesn't know it, but he's acting under post-hypnotic orders, electrically generated. I'm not stepping out of line: I am merely exacting what is just and right. Bob will go through all the necessary legal moves to repay that money out of mother's will because he's incapable of doing anything else."

Betty and Dick glanced but took no further notice. To the mind of a child money does not mean a thing.

"But your mother was worth a fortune!" Emily whispered, her eyes brightening. "Why, Albert dear, this solves everything! We can have a new house, a new cooker, all, the labor-saving devices we should have had long ago, and—"

"No," Albert interrupted, seating himself.

"What do you mean—no? Aren't we entitled to those things?"

"Entitled maybe, but they'll have to wait until later on. You'll get them in time, and a good deal else besides—but this money is needed for something much more important. That is why I went to so much trouble getting hold of it."

"And what is more important than the comfort of the

family?"

"A guided missile."

"What on earth do you mean by that?"

"I mean that I want a guided missile, or rather the materials to construct one. I know exactly how to do it, thanks to studying things out at the laboratory—and I won't be contravening orders either if I construct an experimental guided missile of my own. Anybody can do it if they want. It's not stealing an invention, a copyright, or anything like that."

Emily swallowed something. "And you mean to tell me—"

"I mean to tell you that, to further my master plan, I must have a guided missile. A really good one manufactured by precision engineers with all the refinements that cost a whale of a lot of money—infinitely more than even Bob's entire fortune. But the kind of rough-and-ready machine that I want can be made for much less, and will be. That's all there is to it."

"This," Emily breathed direfully, "is about the finish! You dangle all that money under my nose, and then whip it away so you can build a rocket, or something. I won't stand for it!"

"What, then, *do* you propose to do?"

Emily clenched her fists and her color deepened— but at length, just as Albert had known from the start, she relaxed again. But there was a suspicion of moisture in her eyes. Never in her life had she been so bitterly disappointed. Albert gave a rather taut smile and clapped an arm about her heavy shoulders.

"Don't let it get you down, Emmy. I'm not throwing the money away, believe me. It'll prove the best investment I ever made insofar that, in the end, it will bring us all the money we need."

"But Albert, of what possible *use* is a guided missile? Where are you going to send it? The moon?"

"No. I'll leave the exploration of outer space to the government and technicians. I've other ideas, ideas such as no man ever had before. You'll see...."

And to this Albert did not add any more. He continued with his normal work day by day, his manner towards his family suggesting that he was secretly satisfied with everything in general; and exactly as he had forecast, his brother reversed his legal chicanery and had the money transferred to Albert's bank after a fortnight's interval. Albert then went to work on purchases from various engineering and precision instrument firms. The sum total of his purchases resolved itself into a seemingly endless stream of crates and packages that were delivered to the outhouse and there left to Albert's ministrations.

To his family he did not explain a thing, and they all knew better than to question him. Every evening, most of the nights, and all through the weekends he tinkered with the equipment, building something complex that looked exactly like a gigantic sewing machine shuttle.

Finally it was Vera who investigated. Since she had once been the victim of her father's peculiar "clock" machine, she felt she was best fitted to be the inquirer for the family, and this decision came at the end of a month of wondering what the head of the household was up to.

"No objections to my coming in here, dad?" Vera asked, as she ventured into the workshop-*cum*-laboratory one evening.

Her father glanced up from a detailed print he was studying. He looked tired from long hours of concentration, but there appeared to be no resentment in his expression.

"Come in if you like, but don't touch anything."

"I wouldn't dream of it." Vera glanced about her at the bewildering array of scientific equipment. "Amazing what you can cram into the small space of this outhouse, isn't it?"

"Mmm."

Vera wandered until she found a stool. She settled on it and folded her arms, watching her father at work. At length he caught her out in gazing.

"Frankly, Vee, I don't like being watched at my work," he said bluntly. "Not that I'm doing anything I shouldn't, but I hate being supervised—and especially by my own daughter."

"Sorry, dad. Believe it or not, though, I'm interested. It just shows how wrong we've all been about you. We thought you were just a grub-along old boy with no ambitions—and now you've got all this junk. Makes you *look* like Edison even if there's nothing more than the comparison."

"Plenty more will happen, m'girl, and don't you forget it!"

"Such as? I don't want to sound like a tiresome child. I'm genuinely interested. Anybody of my generation would be. Mum says you're building a guided missile. Am I a nuisance if I ask you why?"

"I am building it," Albert answered vaguely, "because I have no other means of becoming an interstellar visitor."

Vera looked puzzled, and then annoyed. She asked no more questions, realizing that her father was being deliberately evasive. So instead she watched him fixing an apparatus like a radio receiver in the center of the giant shuttle.

"That to control it?" she questioned, coming across to the projectile and surveying it.

"Uh-huh."

"And what's this other thing for? Like a tape recorder on a small scale."

"That's exactly what it is—a tape recorder. Only instead of a ribbon coated with magnetic oxide I have a length of film with a track."

"Sound track, you mean? What does it say?"

"Never mind," Albert countered, and continued with his task until at last Vera wearied of his obstructionist tactics and returned into the house to report to her mother. Albert smiled to himself and wondered what kind of a hash the unscientific Vera would make of her explanation.

He for his part continued working as usual far into the night. He returned into the house for supper, sidetracked all the questions which were aimed at him, and so finally returned to his task.

It was towards three in the morning when he had the rocket projectile's internal workings completed. To seal the outer casing was easy. This done, he gave the projectile a final glance, and went out into the garden and surveyed the night scene. Everybody in the house had gone to bed and so apparently had the neighbors. There was only the dark of the early hours, a cold wind, and the lofty, hazy dome of the stars.

"Perfect," Albert murmured. "Test number one."

Returning into the workshop, he wheeled it out on the portable ramp he had made for the projectile, and presently he had the rocket tilted at the required pre-determined diagonal angle. Albert returned to the safety of his workshop and activated the control that fired the single rear jet. With a brief blinding glare and roar and a blast of super-hot air the small missile started to climb towards the stars, the line of fire marking its flight slowly becoming smaller to Albert's watching eyes.

He settled himself at the radio control devices he had created. Upon a television screen there appeared a solitary white circle. This circle was actually within the projectile itself, being photographed by an automatic television pick-up eye. It showed Albert that the projectile was still in good shape and climbing fast.

Another instrument produced verification of this, translating in terms of radio the height the projectile had reached.

"Perfect!" Albert whispered. "Now let's see...."

He switched in the remote control apparatus at the moment when, according to his calculations, the initial fuel supply of the projectile would exhaust itself. Here was the point where radio took over, guiding the projectile onwards towards the rim of the atmosphere and finally, Albert hoped, into the gulf of space itself.

CHAPTER FOUR

Completely absorbed in his task, Albert snapped another switch. This operated a second television pickup within the rocket and gave back a view as seen from the rocket itself. It showed the stars; then as Albert angled the view around somewhat, he beheld in the screen a patchwork of lights that was presumably the earthly landscape where cities blazed in the night.

Higher and higher went his rocket. Forty miles—a hundred. The controlling apparatus, homemade though it was, was functioning perfectly. And now that the projectile's exhaust had died out there was no clue as to what was happening. This, to Albert, was the most important matter of all.

Still he remained at his task, inflicting upon himself the most exacting hour of work he had ever known. But at the end of it the instruments told him one thing: the rocket had traveled way out beyond Earth and, by pre-calculation, proceeded to pursue an orbit of its own. Therefore it no longer required controlling. It retained the velocity it had originally possessed since it was in free space and—all control removed—was now hurtling around the Earth, after the fashion of an invisible satellite.

Albert chuckled to himself and sat back in his chair. Inside that rocket were instruments that could make him the master of the world. And not only that: he could, he believed, compel men and women everywhere to do exactly as he commanded.

Soon he would know for certain.

He did not explain himself to his family when they asked where the guided missile had gone; nor did he put his main purpose into action for many weeks after dispatching the rocket. He wanted the "hue and cry" of his family to die down. But at length he felt it was safe enough to experiment—so, just over a month after launching the rocket, he entered his workshop-laboratory and put the instruments in operation. They gave him exactly the answer he hoped for. The rocket was still pursuing its orbit round the Earth, traveling at thousands of miles an hour.

"Now," Albert murmured, "let us see if the great idea will work...."

He opened a switch and closed it again. That was all.

This done, he cut off all the power and strolled back into the house. Emily, his wife, was in the kitchen armchair as usual. The younger end was entirely absent. Albert lighted a cigarette, strolled to the radio, and switched it on.

"Do we *have* to listen to that?" Emily cocked an eye on him. "I'm just enjoying this romance—"

"Romance! I thought you'd outgrown that sort of nonsense long ago! *I* want the radio, and I mean to have it. Any more objections?"

Emily sank lower in her chair and went on reading. She had that queer gift of being able to detach herself from everything else whilst she read, hence the popular music blaring forth did not disturb her in the least. Albert stood by the window, not seeing the view outside, his whole attention concentrated upon the radio.

Then suddenly it came! A voice! And *what* a voice! It was arresting, resonant, and richly bass. Every word was absolutely distinct; every syllable clearly articulated. It was the voice of a man of obvious personality. It was the voice of a Conqueror!

"People of the world called Earth, listen! I command that you listen! Listen, I say! *Listen!*"

Albert swung from the window in apparent surprise. Emily found her concentration shattered and stared blankly at the radio, the normal program having been swamped. No, not *entirely* swamped. It was still there in the background, a ghost of its former self, like a band on the edge of infinity. For the moment the Voice had ceased, and instead the soft rush of power in the speaker bespoke a strong transmission overlapping the normal radio band.

"Did—did somebody really say that?" Emily asked sharply, glancing up at Albert as he came level with her.

"Somebody did, yes."

"Sure it wasn't you? Sure you haven't fixed some kind of gadget to the radio?"

"Don't be ridiculous, Emmy! When did *my* voice ever sound like that? As for doing something to the radio, look at it for yourself."

"That wouldn't do any good. You know I don't understand radio sets—"

"People of Earth, attention!"

The Voice again, and this time there was no mistaking it. Emily sat transfixed, staring at the radio. Not that she was the only one who stared. Everywhere where radio was tuned in, throughout the world, the Voice had wiped out normal transmission in order to make itself heard.

"People of Earth, I speak to you in English because, as far as I can ascertain, it is the language mainly used throughout your planet. Those of you who do not understand my words must have them translated for the sake of other races.... I bring to you a message— and it is a message of cheer; but there is also a warning. I can destroy or uplift you at will because I am infinitely more intelligent than you. I come from far-away Andromeda. I am watching you, studying you, just as your own scientists would study an insect under an electron microscope."

"Gosh!" Emily gulped, in the brief pause, and Albert put an arm about her shoulders as he waited for the next.

"The message of cheer is this: end your differences with each other. Tear down the barriers that would destroy peace on your planet. Bury suspicion. Seize each other's hands in friendship, if that be your signification of mutual trust. And my *warning* is this: if you do not overcome your warlike tendencies, your crimes, your diseases, and your villainies, I shall destroy you. Not slowly, not a few at a time, but in one flash of cosmic energy. Believe me, I have it in my control to bend the forces of the cosmos to my will and, rather than have a planet infested with warring, fighting legions—such as you seem to be—I intend to use that power to the full...."

"He—he has a lovely voice," Emily muttered. "Sort of soothes you, doesn't it?"

"The voice of a master mind," Albert murmured. "The voice of a conqueror—"

"I know that this communication will throw you into confusion," the Voice resumed. "For that reason I do not expect action from you one way or the other until some little time has elapsed. In one week from today I shall speak again, and I shall know by then from your radio broadcasts whether or not you have decided to heed the messages I have given you. Remember my power, but do not force me to use it."

The Voice faded suddenly, and with it came the resumption of the music that had been in the background. But almost immediately the music was faded out and the normal announcer came through.

"Stand by, everybody, for an important announcement. Stand by, please." And, after a pause: "Not two minutes ago there just ceased an experimental radio amateur seeking a new way to obtain publicity, and you are asked—those of you who heard the messages—

to ignore them completely They are quite without meaning and are obviously intended as a build-up to some big radio presentation—"

"The damned, abysmal idiot!" Albert breathed, in sudden unexpected fury.

"Those of you who did not hear the mystery broadcast might wish to have the details, so here is a recording of the message exactly as it was received."

Thereupon the Voice spoke again in exact repetition. Albert stood with his fists clenched, listening. Emily gave him a troubled glance now and again until at length the recording was over.

"We are asked to repeat our assurance that there is absolutely no foundation whatever for believing— and even less obeying—the commands given by this hoaxer. Our engineers are already at work tracing the origin of the broadcast, and the law will do the rest. Now our normal service will resume with—"

Albert switched off, glaring at Emily as though she had been personally responsible for the announcer's summing-up.

"Hoax indeed!" Albert laughed shortly. "They'll think very differently before long, believe me. What did *you* think? Did it sound like a hoax to you? Be absolutely frank, Emmy."

"You want the absolute truth?"

"I just said so, didn't I?"

Emily reflected. "Matter of fact, I thought it was all very compelling. That's a wonderful voice you've managed to use, but it's going to get you into hot water before you're finished. You shouldn't *do* such things, Albert!"

"What! Great heavens, woman, you don't suppose that *I* sent that message, do you? How could I when I was here all the time?"

"I don't know how, but I noticed you suddenly decided to have the radio on whereas usually you never listen to it—or the TV either—and instead bury yourself in those science magazines. I also remember you once saying that you'd enforce peace on earth and lots of other silly, impossible things. Even if I'm not wonderfully bright, I'm not an absolute fool either. You *fixed* that voice somehow, but I haven't the brains to work it out."

Albert sighed. "Well anyway, Emmy, it wasn't my voice. You should know that. I've a thin, high tone, and no power on earth could give it that resonant quality—that air of command."

"Then maybe you hired an actor or an elocutionist, recorded the message on a tape machine, and then broadcast it from the outhouse."

Albert grinned widely, which only served to make Emily downright cross.

"From the outhouse!" Albert exclaimed, raising his hands helplessly. "Just how limited can your imagination be?"

"It isn't limited at all! Vera said you had a tape recording gadget in there when you were making that missile thing—so it sort of seems logical to me."

"I only hope you are typical, m'dear. Yes," Albert

admitted, "I *am* the brains behind the Voice, but I am not the Voice itself. Nor do I fear detector-engineers, the law, or anything else. Just how I've accomplished my little trick I don't propose to explain. I just want to sit back and watch the scientific wiseacres tear themselves to pieces trying to work this one out. I've been laughed at for long enough by all and sundry: now it is my turn to laugh. And believe me, this is only the start."

"I—I thought you'd planned something by electric hypnosis? Like the stunt you played on Vera. What has the Voice got to do with it?"

"Everything, as you'll see later. This scheme is the work of years, Emmy—dovetailed and complete. I am already the master of this planet, and yet I am also an obscure laboratory janitor, the last person to be suspected. That is, providing you and the kids keep quiet."

"*I* will," Emily promised quickly, "but I can't be expected to answer for Vee. She knows more of your activities than I do."

Albert reflected. "It might be a good idea to destroy her memory in regard to what she knows about me. That's quite easy by electrical hypnosis, and harmless. I'll have to think it over. She's a headstrong girl and might not listen to an ordinary appeal for silence. I'll tackle her when she comes home."

Upon which Albert relaxed into a chair and, lighting a cigarette, he sat thinking. He wondered if his announcement via ether had made any impression in other countries, since it appeared that England was going to treat the whole thing as a joke.

Truth to tell, however, England was *not* taking the message as a joke. This slant on the business had only been thrown out to allay possible public panic. A message like that could very easily stampede the weaker-willed members of the community, so instant disavowal had been decided upon, both by the governors of the radio-television system and the responsible high-ups of the government.

Behind the scenes, however, there was chaos. When the first message had come through, startled engineers had glanced at their monitor speakers relaying the normal program and had then, with commendable presence of mind, switched in the recording equipment and taken the message down. Hurried phone calls and consultations had followed, checking with other radio engineers in various parts of the country.

Yes, the message was being received all over Britain. Yes, Europe was getting it. America—Canada—the Orient—ships at sea—aircraft—the borders of the Arctic and Antarctic Circles. Everywhere a radio was alive the mellow, commanding voice was being heard, overpowering all normal transmissions.

"Get a detector on that interference!" commanded the wrathful voice of the governor of the BBC.

"Trace that hoaxer who's shooting his face off!" ordered the Controller of America's biggest television network.

Other directors and controllers said the same thing

in their various languages, and for the duration of the messages the backroom boys of the world's radio stations behaved like ants whose hill has been over-turned.

In the English stations frenzied engineers carefully tuned in their detectors and made readings. Radar beams were radiated to all points of the compass—and above—but only from overhead was there any response. There followed hurried checking with other stations, and the consensus of reports showed that in every case the reading came from the sky. That meant an airplane—or did it? When eventually a computa-tion of the message's source had been arrived at, it was found to be from outer space.

Later that evening, the chief engineer of British Radio Network held an emergency conference with his colleagues.

"The only other answer is that it came from outer space," another engineer confirmed. "But no govern-ment in the world capable of putting a craft into space has admitted responsibility, so—"

"That being, or whatever he is, said he came from Andromeda," the chief said. "But the whole thing's so utterly inconceivable! A being from Andromeda who talks perfect English telling us what to do! In any case, radio signals from another galaxy would be thousands of years old when they reached us!"

"Not if he's traveled here by spaceship," someone observed dryly.

"Hardly likely, is it? It's obviously a hoax, and a

damned clever one. Get the observatories on the radio. If there really is an alien spaceship above the Earth, then the telescopes and radar defence systems may have picked him up."

So the call went forth—to Mount Wilson, to the big observatories of the Eastern world, to Greenwich, to all observation stations where the night had come. Harassed astronomers checked their plates from the previous night; others studied those that had been photographed that selfsame hour, but in no case was there a sign of a spaceship, or a masking of the stars that might point to the presence of a dark object between them and Earth.

"Are we barking up the wrong tree?" demanded the chief radio engineer of the superintendent of Mount Wilson, where was sited the biggest telescope on Earth. "Would it be possible for you to *see* a spaceship at, say, a hundred thousand miles' distance?"

"It would depend on its size, of course," came the reply over six thousand miles of ether, "but if it should be of a size usually expected of space machines, then we'd be able to see it. Only we haven't."

"Any other suggestions, then? Could a being from outer space live in the void by himself, without a space-ship, and thereby be too small to be visible?"

"Anything is possible when considering a being who can travel here from Andromeda! I can imagine a creature being able to exist in the infinite zero of space, not needing to draw breath, probably relying on cosmic energy for his existence."

"And such a person might be intelligent? Might understand radio and how to operate it?"

"More than likely. We of Earth are by no means the ultimate in intelligence."

"Mmm—thanks. It's interesting even if it doesn't help any."

Irritated, the chief switched off and turned to look at his colleagues. They were scowling in thought, trying to knock some sense into the mystery that had suddenly descended upon them.

"No luck there," the chief said. "No spaceship. The only possibility, if we don't admit a hoax, is a being able to live in an absolute vacuum of unimaginable cold and carry radio equipment about with him."

"Bosh!" one of the engineers declared flatly.

The chief returned to his chair and studied his notes. Then he said: "There is also this matter of power. Somehow he has produced enough of it to swamp all ordinary radio waves and send his own message on full power over thousands of miles of space! That's the devil of a lot of power no matter how you look at it."

One of the men raised an eyebrow. "How about *atomic* power? It's the *multum in parvo* when it comes to terrific concentration of energy in a small space. If this unknown is as clever as he makes himself out to be, atomic power may present no problem to him. He could contrive all the energy needed in a very small compass."

"Could be," the chief muttered, musing. "Pity the message has stopped. Some of the scientific laboratories could have directed Geiger counters along the radio beam to see if there is a radioactive response."

"Over *that* distance! Couldn't be done, chief. We haven't equipment that sensitive."

Long silence, each man refusing to admit to himself that the possibility of a being in outer space was logical; yet if it was not logical, what was the real answer? The engineers became gradually more infuriated that they could not think of one.

And throughout the night the wrangling and the arguments and the theories continued, but even the best brains in science could not think of the answer— which was probably one reason why Albert Simpkins slept with a blissful smile on his face. For a man considered to be a congenital idiot to have baffled the world's cleverest scientists was certainly something.

Next morning the newspapers had plenty to say. Exercising the freedom of the press, they did not wrap things up in cotton wool, as had the radio chiefs. They came straight out with their opinions, and very pungent they were.

The *Daily Truth* declared outright in its leader that it believed the advent of the interspacial being was absolutely genuine, and demanded that the people of the world heed what had been said and prepare itself to receive the benefits which had been promised for the cessation of international hostility.

Unfortunately, however, the *Daily Truth* was a lone voice crying in the wilderness, for in the main the newspapers poured ridicule on the whole business. Some of them did so from choice; others were compelled to through governmental pressure. It was still considered unsafe to admit to the public that there might be something in the remarkable business.

Theories were put forward, some supported by proof, to show how illogical the mystery voice was. Famous men gave their opinions, and from the rubbish they wrote it was plain they did not know what they were talking about. And the men and women of the world, including Albert Simpkins, went to work as usual and discussed the amazing business with each other.

Albert found the laboratory staff particularly interesting that morning. They were striving by every means they knew to arrive at something worthwhile to explain the voice of the Andromedian. The government had ordered that they dish up something to satisfy the unconvinced public, for to tell Mr. and Mrs. John Citizen that the whole thing was a hoax was not enough. Proof of this was urgently needed.

"To my mind," said one of the senior technicians, within Albert's hearing, as he mopped the floor, "there's only one way to ever get at the truth, and that is to go into outer space and establish contact with this Andromedian. To judge from his message he's friendly enough so that's one good thing."

"And the least important," another pointed out. "Jumping into outer space isn't just something you can decide upon and then do."

"Then we've got to get to work on it! The government wants action, and it's up to us to provide it."

Albert glanced up. "Not my business, gents," he said humbly, "but what good do you suppose it would do you if you fly into space to look for our friend?"

"What good!" the senior technician echoed. "I should have thought that was plain enough. We'll prove that the man with the voice really exists—and that is the point which so far is not settled."

Albert gave a sigh. "Seems sort of queer to me, gents. You are willing to risk your lives diving into outer space, and if you find the man from Andromeda you'll simply come back and tell the public he's there. You certainly will not change his plans. He means what he says. All it amounts to is your risking your necks to satisfy a lot of fools who won't—or can't—believe."

"Maybe he's got something there," one of the scientists commented, glancing at his colleagues.

"Take me now," Albert continued, with a forlorn glance. "I'm typical of the average man. Wife, family, menial job, low wage. I'm told a story by the government, and I accept it as true. I don't expect fellows like you, who are needed by the scientific world, to go risking your lives to prove to me that the voice is the real thing and not a trick. That's how all men and women should accept things, and because I'm typical I know what I'm talking about."

With which Albert went on with his mopping, careful not to say too much. He had done his best to delay the plans of the scientists, even if he had not stopped them altogether. In any case, as he well knew, the matter of manned space travel was a colossal project that would take time to mount. On the other hand there were guided missiles, but the possibility of one of them photographing his own projectile circling the Earth thousands of miles away was most unlikely. Such an occurrence would rely on the two projectiles being within photographic range of each other at a given moment—which extreme improbability made Albert smile to himself and hum a tune as he worked....

That evening when he returned home, he appeared subdued. Since on every hand he had seen the forces of science and the Press marshalling themselves against the mystery voice, this was not surprising, but most certainly he did not intend to admit he had started something he could not finish.

"I don't see much sign of the nations of the world extending the hand of friendship," Emily commented acidly, serving up fried fish. "There seems to be more commotion than ever. You should have let sleeping dogs lie; that's what I say."

"Since that would entail no effort, your reaction is understandable," Albert commented. "Anyway, I didn't expect the nations to suddenly kiss each other. These things take time. At the end of the week that I stipulated, I'll send another message, and implement it with action. You see if I don't."

Emily shook her head as she rolled herself into her chair at the table. "Playing with fire, Albert; that's what you're doing. You've got the whole world yelling."

"I know—but I've got it baffled as well. You just don't know how much of a kick I get out of that."

The conversation ceased as Vera came in from business. It had been safe to talk before Dick and Betty—Ethel being at a party—but Vera was a different matter.

"Getting quite a lot of second-hand publicity, dad, aren't you?" she asked dryly, when presently she was settled at the table. "Everybody everywhere is talking about the Voice."

"From which I gather you believe I'm responsible for it?"

"Of course you are! Besides, mum told me everything you told her last evening."

Albert's eyes strayed to his wife, but she busied herself in dissecting fish from a backbone. Then he moved his gaze back to his daughter and met the look of challenge in her bright hazel eyes.

"Matter of fact," Vera said frankly, "I think the whole thing's cowardly, dad. Since you're back of everything, why don't you come into the open and say so?"

"The sooner you stop taking things for granted, my girl, as your mother does, the better! I have admitted that I am responsible for the Voice's message being sent to the world, but I am *not* the Voice itself. That is something different."

A sullen look spread over Vera's face. Deep down in her mind there was still a smoldering resentment for the way she had been made the victim of her father's original experiment in electrical hypnosis.

"Seen tonight's *Sentinel*?" she asked, and as her father and mother shook their heads, she added: "The scientific branch of Scotland Yard has taken the unusual step of offering fifty thousand pounds reward to anybody who can give information which can lead to the police interviewing last night's hoaxer."

"If that isn't an admission of failure, I don't know what is," Albert commented. Then he reflected for a moment. "Fifty thousand pounds, eh? A fair sum for the authorities to offer. Shows they are pretty desperate for information."

"Naturally they are! Look at the upset the Voice has caused! In some places people have panicked; money markets have turned a somersault; international relationships have been made rockier than they were before. There's no end to the upheaval, and it looks as though it will get gradually worse. That sort of thing has got to be stopped at any price."

Albert smiled inscrutably to himself and continued eating his fish.

"Fifty thousand pounds," Vera said, pondering, "is quite a nice sum of money. I know Hal and I would find it pretty useful, anyway—"

CHAPTER FIVE

Albert started, and so did Emily. Vera met the two pairs of eyes with brazen calmness.

"I've earned some kind of reward for the way you treated me with that machine of yours, dad," she said presently. "Without so much as a by-your-leave you made a chump out of me—and I haven't forgotten it. Fifty thousand pounds would just about compensate me for my injured dignity."

"You little fool!" Emily snapped. "Don't you dare go telling tales to the police or you know what you'll get!"

"I'll get fifty thousand pounds, and my information will be well worth it, too. An outhouse stuffed with electrical gadgets; a machine which reads brain emanations and then puts people through their paces whether they like it or not. Frankly, I'd have gone to the police on my way home, only I wanted to give you fair warning first, dad."

"Nice of you!" Albert's eyes were glinting. "How much good does a warning do me? I can't stop you going—except by force, and that would bring the police just the same."

"The way out," Vera said, "is to stop fooling about

with this dangerous game you're playing. I'm saying that for your own good—as your daughter, as one who sees what sort of havoc you have created, and will still create. Just promise to stop, and I'll keep quiet."

"I do believe," Albert said slowly, "that in a round-about way you're acting in what you think are my best interests."

"Of course I am. If I were not, I'd have collected that reward and be hanged to you!"

Long pause. Emily waited, glancing from father to daughter; then gradually the anger died out of Albert's expression, and he smiled.

"The trouble is, Vee, you don't know precisely what I'm aiming at, or what good I intend to bestow. After tea I'll show you."

"All right." Vera shrugged. "But you'll have to be mighty convincing."

Vaguely, Emily wondered what Albert was driving at, but she asked no questions, and the tea proceeded without the matter of the Voice being raised again. Immediately it was over, Albert motioned Vera ahead of him, and together they went into the laboratory-outhouse in the garden. Accustomed to having been here before, Vera waited, her arms folded, as her father examined his equipment carefully. Finally he made a setting on his "clock-*cum*-hypnosis" machine and switched on the power.

"This will give you some idea of what I'm driving at, Vee," he explained. "Now, as an instance. At the moment you don't know how to play a concerto, do you?"

"Huh?" Vera looked astonished. "Play a concerto? I can't even play at *all*, and you know it!"

"Normally you cannot sing either, yet you became a prima donna whilst under electrical compulsion. This time I want you to feel the power of this apparatus in a different way—to be conscious of what is happening to you instead of being blacked-out during the process. As you feel the power of great music stealing into you, think how the sudden acquirement of talents and gifts will affect other people. Think of the medical men making amazing discoveries for the relief of human suffering; think of the down-and-outs finding they have rare gifts which can make their fortunes.... Those are only a few of the things I intend to bequeath to humanity."

Vera was silent, aware that the strange instrument was directly facing her. In her inmost heart she trusted her father, but she was not too sanguine about his scientific accomplishments. Then it gradually dawned upon her that she was not in the laboratory any more. She was in the kitchen, flat out on the old chesterfield. Her father and mother were bending over her anxiously. From a corner Dick and Betty were watching in wide-eyed wonder.

"What—what happened?" Vera asked slowly, rising up and holding her spinning head.

"You just came over queer whilst you were having tea," Albert explained gently. "You'll be all right. I should go to bed if I were you. If you're no better in the morning I'll call a doctor."

"Yes—thanks." Vera felt as though the room were spinning round in circles as she got groggily to her feet. "I'll be better in bed—I hope."

Albert jerked his head briefly to his wife, and watched as she piloted the unsteady girl from the room. Presently there were sounds in the bedroom above. Albert listened to them and tightened his lips as he stared absently through the window onto the spring evening.

"What's the matter with Vee, daddy?" Betty asked, coming over.

Albert pushed a hand through her dark curls. "Nothing, love. She'll be all right—"

"Did she fall in the garden? Why did you have to carry her in? Was she sick?"

"Yes, sick," Albert muttered. "But it needn't worry you, Betty. Go back and play your game—"

Emily returned to the kitchen, her flabby face troubled. She put a hand on Albert's arm.

"Albert, don't you think that you're going too far? She's really ill!"

"Only nervous shock, and it'll be gone in an hour or two. I *had* to do it, Emmy! Don't you see?" He lowered his voice and looked at her intensely. "I had to destroy her memory concerning my activities. From now on she will not remember a thing about my experiments— and that outhouse must always be kept locked. I have so much to accomplish, I can't allow Vee to upset my plans. Nor you, Emmy. Remember that...."

Emily nodded silently but did not say anything—and Vera recovered later exactly as her father had predicted. She was manifestly puzzled by what had happened to her, but nonetheless she appeared willing to accept the explanation that something she had eaten had violently disagreed with her. Certainly she did not evince any further interest in her father's activities, which was all that mattered to him. He fitted a special burglar-proof lock to his "laboratory" and took good care it was always in operation when he was not around.

The week stipulated by the Voice passed by without any sign of change in the crazy ways of Mankind, so on the seventh night after his original message Albert went into the workshop, opened and closed a switch, and then returned into the house to listen to the radio. Emily, guessing what was coming, merely looked at him and did not say anything.

And for the second time that mellow, mysterious voice boomed forth on an astonished world, swamping normal radio programs exactly as before.

"Apparently you do not see fit to heed the communication I gave you, my friends, which is indeed to be regretted. I do realize, however, that you probably find my presence hard to credit, and therefore I must give you some sign to prove that my powers are all that I claim them to be. You will shortly find that four famous financiers in Britain will hand over to deserving charities vast sums of money of their own free will. When you observe the identities of these financiers, you will believe, as I intend that you should, that a miracle has happened. After that, watch for other unusual events in your social order. In time I will speak to you again and see if you have learned your lesson. One thing you must remember—just as I can force the dispensation of good deeds, so I can force the power of destruction. Settle your differences now and live in peace, whilst there is still time."

The Voice ceased. Back of the broadcasting stations the frantic investigations of the previous occasion had begun—destined to produce the same desolation of results as before. Albert grinned to himself and met Emily's eyes as the message faded into silence and the surge of power in the speaker stopped.

"Good, eh?" he asked, smiling.

"If you can implement your pledge, I suppose it is. And that reminds me: you said you would bring thousands of pounds into our lap as time advanced. I don't see any sign of that happening. Your message speaks of deserving charities, so I'd remind you that charity begins at home."

"I'll come to that in its proper order. It wouldn't be good policy on my part if I suddenly became the possessor of really large sums of money. It would set people—and ultimately the police—thinking."

"Up to you. Not a thing I can do about it. I certainly would like to know how you produce this Voice business though, and with such terrific power."

"So would a lot of other people. Maybe I'll explain it one day. Right now I've things to do—" Albert headed for the door and then paused, glancing back over his shoulder. "By the way, I quit my job today. I forgot to tell you."

"Quit your job! But what do we use for money?"

"We've enough to get by with for the time being. I'll soon provide more. The point is, now my master plan is in definite operation, I'll have to have a good deal more time to myself. I have four financiers to visit for one thing, starting tonight. Don't worry, Emmy; everything will work out all right."

Perhaps, though, Albert would not have sounded—or have felt—so sanguine had he been present at that moment in the Scientific Division of Scotland Yard. Here the biggest experts in scientific investigation were grouped, summoned hastily the moment the second message had commenced. Now they sat debating in the Assistant Commissioner's office, listening at the same time to the recording of the message that had been made.

The first man to speak was Grant Forsythe, an up-and-coming fortyish man with a profound grasp of scientific essentials. His unusual knack of looking beyond the immediate aspect of a scientific problem had brought him in recent years to the front rank of the Division.

"I'll stake everything I've got that the owner of that Voice is not an interstellar being from Andromeda," he said; and the other men looked at him.

"We're all willing to stake that," the Assistant Commissioner replied, "but the trouble is, we can't prove it."

"In that message," Forsythe continued, pondering, "I see the first signs of a clue. We have been told, by this supposed intergalactic being, that he is all-powerful, that he can understand our radio system, our language, and everything else. Right?"

The assembled men nodded, waiting interestedly.

"Why, then, in his message did the being say that we 'probably' find his presence hard to credit? 'Probably' implies that there is a doubt about it. If, as he says, he can understand our radio messages, he must know from the broadcasts of the past week that we certainly *do* find his presence hard to credit."

"Proving what?" questioned the A.C.

"Proving this, I think: that the being spoke that message before he knew of our reaction and that led him to instinctively say 'probably.' He was endeavoring to be wise before the event. I submit that an all-powerful being has no need to consider anything as 'probable.' He *knows!*"

Livened interest came to the faces around the table. One of the Division leaned forward earnestly.

"Are you suggesting a *recorded* message, Grant? Is that your angle?"

"That's my angle, yes. Why shouldn't the latest message, and the one before it, have been recorded at the same time, the man who did the talking guessing full well that, in the beginning, nobody would believe him—hence the element of doubt in message number two. I know it's a hair-thin foundation to work on, but I think it's better than nothing."

"And the Voice comes from above—a hundred thousand miles away. Don't forget that."

"I'm not doing, but that fact doesn't make me believe any more strongly in an interstellar being. There's another point, too. Had this creature said he was speaking from Mars or Venus, or even the Moon, I'd have been more likely to credit it. But to suggest Andromeda is ridiculous! That famous Nebula is untold light-centuries distant from us, and unless this being has eternal life, or can travel faster than light, he could never make the journey from Andromeda to here in anything like what we call a lifetime."

"I'd thought of that, too," admitted the A.C., musing. "But again I say we must have *proof.* We can theorize until we're black in the face, but it doesn't get us anywhere."

Forsythe reflected for a moment or two. He was a bull-necked, arrogant little man in appearance, yet soft-voiced and gentle in manner—a living contradiction in fact. Finally, after a long spell of cogitation, he aimed his sharp blue eyes back to the waiting A.C.

"Whoever is back of this is obviously a scientist of no mean order, and therefore it seems to me that it is amongst the ranks of the scientists where we have to start searching. We have a lead on this occasion, because four famous financiers have been marked down for the Being's attention. In this country there are seven top-line financiers, so I suggest that every one of them be watched night and day, and if anybody strange communicates with any of them, we'll step in and do some questioning."

The A.C. nodded his approval. "Good idea; I'll get men on it."

"I'm quite sure we have to get it into our heads that we're dealing with somebody right here on this planet of ours and not with a mastermind from Andromeda," Forsythe continued. "As to the trick of producing a Conqueror's Voice from outer space—well, there are scientific ways of doing that, too, but we can leave it for the moment. Fortunately, this unknown seems to be generously inclined at the moment, though I certainly doubt that he'll establish the peace on earth towards which he seems to be striving."

"It appears," the A.C. commented, "that you have a deeper grasp of this complex business than the rest of us, so maybe you'd better take over the job exclusively. You have *carte blanche* to do exactly as you see fit to get to the bottom of this mystery."

"Right!" Forsythe gave a nod. "I'll do my best, sir—and the first move must be to keep a watch on the seven top-line financiers. I'm pretty sure that will get us somewhere."

And it was at this time that Albert Simpkins was in the region of Maida Vale, his queer clock-and-hypnosis machine supported from his shoulder by a leather strap. As usual he looked exactly like an itinerant musician without his monkey, or else a photographer carrying an unusually large camera case. He hummed cheerfully to himself as he ambled along, nor did he hesitate for a moment as presently he passed a police officer on the beat.

"Nice evening, officer!"

"Very nice, sir. We can do with plenty like these. All the summer before us." Albert grinned and continued on his way, pausing when he reached one of those secluded recreation grounds that are legion. Here he spent some time studying a map, upon which he had already drawn concentric circles to make his "aim" with the hypnosis beam infallible. He already knew the brain frequencies of the four financiers he had selected, having obtained them during the past week.

It had been a simple job. First he had enquired over the phone if each man was at business or away from home—and by good fortune each one had been on the spot. On the plea of important information concerning stock reports, he had made four consecutive appointments with each man to fit into his own lunch hour when he had been a laboratory cleaner.... His four interviews had yielded nothing from the stock and share angle, but in his pocket his stop-watch detector had operated four times—a smaller instrument than the first one he had devised, and especially useful for "undercover" work.

Thus, knowing each frequency, the rest was easy. If in each case there was a reaction on his apparatus, it meant that the financier concerned was involuntarily being impregnated with electrical hypnosis—and from a distance of not quite two miles. Albert had worked out the distance to a mathematical certainty, which—although he was unaware of it—was something the

Scientific Division had not thought of. Hence, although they had watching plainclothes men keeping unnoticed surveillance over seven different financiers, nothing unusual was observed.

And Albert trotted from one point to the other in the spring evening, his only delay being in the case of the last of the four, for whom he had to wait until 10:30 before he could establish contact with him. This accomplished, he returned home, and the p.c. men on duty yawned and wondered when—if ever—anything was likely to happen.

That they were discomfited on the afternoon of the following day is to state it mildly. Every one of them was recalled from observation to attend a conference at the Yard. Here they found Grant Forsythe nearly breathing sparks.

"What kind of dummies are you?" he demanded, striding up and down and waving his, hands angrily. "I give you the job of watching the financiers, and none of you sees anything!"

"*None* of us," one of the p.c. men confirmed. "Nothing has happened—so what did we do wrong?"

"Everything, I should think!" Forsythe gave a sour glance. "On the streets this evening the newspapers will carry the news that Carson, Landhurst, Trascon, and Fox—four of the hardest-headed financiers in the city—have *all* given huge sums to charity! The amount involved is in the order of millions."

The assembled men stared blankly.

"Which means," Forsythe continued bitterly, "that

our unknown scientist has kept his word. He said we would regard the donations to charity as something of a miracle, and that is just what they are! The four men concerned have never been known to hand out a penny in their lives before, except for a handsome profit. But, damn me, what's the answer? How did the man do it without ever being seen?"

Since the p.c. men had not the remotest idea they remained silent. Forsythe plunged his hands in his trousers pockets and mooched around the office, brooding.

"I got the tip-off about the financiers from the *Evening Star*," he explained. "That was why I recalled you. No use keeping a watch if this scientist can sneak by under your noses. Or maybe he uses remote control."

"I should think that's very probable," one of the men commented. "I'll gamble the Voice is remote-controlled, so probably everything else is too."

"My job now," Forsythe decided, "is to have a talk with each of these financiers, and try to find out what prompted them to such sudden generosity. If it was done by hypnotism there may be some kind of hang-over...."

And, his mind made up, Forsythe immediately darted off on this new track and whipped up the telephone.... Albert Simpkins, meanwhile, armed with his small detector, was paying a number of apparently meaningless calls on various great public figures, sometimes being given an audience, sometimes not. He had started a kind of wandering campaign which, in the days that followed, impelled him to talk to famous actors and actresses, politicians, doctors, people in the immediate news—anybody and everybody who mattered in the community. His excuse was always the same—he represented a famous daily paper and wanted details for an "exclusive" on this or that famous personality. The flattery never misfired, and since he had no intention of ever returning, he risked the lie by which he gained audience. He took good care, also, to stop before his actions seemed too suspicious.

Not that the police were bothered about a bogus newspaper correspondent: they were too busy trying to trace a clever scientist who was making rings round law and order....

A week passed. Charities were the better off by several million sterling, and Grant Forsythe was scratching the back of his bullet head. The financiers had all said they had performed their acts of generosity out of sheer goodness of heart. No compulsion about it. Whether they were speaking the truth or whether they did not wish it publicised that they were normally tight-fisted, was not clear. Certainly *Forsythe* was no better off. The more he thought about it the more certain he became that to solve the riddle from the surface of the ground was next to impossible—so he turned to that other branch of science, experimental rocketry.

"What," he asked, of the chief scientist of Britain's experimental rocket station, "are the chances of sending a manned rocket to a hundred thousand miles up?"

"Mighty slim," the engineer answered. "Unmanned, yes—anytime you like these days, but with a human being inside I wouldn't guarantee his safety."

"I'd sooner die attempting something than live and be a failure," Forsythe said. "You know why I'm here—because of the Voice. Or rather 'The Conqueror's Voice' as the newspapers are calling it."

"So you said over the phone." The scientist gazed dispassionately. "And not finding any answer you want, to go to the presumed source of the Voice and look for yourself?"

"That's it. If I don't solve this business after having been given all the resources of the Yard's scientific division, I'll finish up without a job. That hasn't got to happen."

"Well, it's not for me to tell you what to do with your own life, Forsythe. I'm simply saying that it's suicide to fly into outer space until every possible contingency has been allowed for. There are the pressures and the strains—"

"Never mind the technical side. Have you got a projectile which, if need be, can carry one man? Myself."

"Dozens of 'em. Experiments with guided missiles are going on all the time. Laboratory 9 can provide one, but you'll have to get legal permission to risk your life."

Forsythe grinned. "Since I represent the law itself, that's a good one! A man doesn't get legal permission to climb a mountain and risk his neck, so I'm not asking anybody if I can risk mine. I'll solve this business no matter what. How long will it take to train me?"

"Hard to say. A few weeks, maybe, with cramming. You'd better go along to Laboratory 9 and see the dean."

Forsythe wasted no time, directed by an inscrutable weaving of circumstances to the very laboratory where Albert Simpkins had learned most of his scientific tricks. But because the lowly Albert had only been a cleaner—and not a very efficient one at that—he was not even mentioned. And for days on end after seeing the dean, Forsythe sweated and struggled to grasp the profound intricacies of a space rocket. It was not the thought of the acclaim that spurred him onwards: it was the ever-driving riddle of the Conqueror's Voice.

And Albert Simpkins went silently about his pre-arranged plans. In his early days, when he had first dabbled with scientific ideas, he had invented quite a few useful gadgets that had since become internationally famous. From ruthless exploiters, who had seen in him the perfect tool, he had received a mere pittance and had not argued. But now he knew the brain frequencies of each of these exploiters, and felt it was time, after an interval of ten years or so, that he reaped his true reward. And he did. Through the simple process of sitting quietly at a spot near to the building containing the man to be "treated," he operated his electric-hypnosis and then went on his way.

The result was surprising. Three famous captains of industry, who had made fortunes out of Albert's original gadgets, suddenly "discovered" simultaneously that there was some hitch in regard to the patent rights, and that Albert had inadvertently been deprived of royalties. In the interval they had accrued to sums that really amounted to something. Would he, to avoid legal complications, accept a reasonable sum in settlement and forget the whole regrettable occurrence?

Albert was only too pleased to be gracious—and, as he had hoped, the news was kept out of the papers by order of the captains of industry, so the fact that he had suddenly become the recipient of thousands of pounds was never made public. At one stroke he had kept his word to Emily—and since Emily loved comfort and money more than anything else on earth, she began to believe there really might be something in this hypnosis-*cum*-Voice business after all.

Still allowing the public to simmer before he inflicted another Voice broadcast, Albert turned his attention to personal matters. He moved to a much larger house where a garage intended for four cars was exactly what he needed for a laboratory. He bought Emily all the electrical gadgets she needed—and then he went into action again, a trifle over three weeks since Broadcast Number 2.

"Peoples of Earth, listen!" And because on that early summer evening it was impossible to do much else when the Voice spoke, everybody with a radio tuned in sat waiting expectantly.

"Peoples of Earth, I have kept my word to you. Four famous financiers have given freely to charity, as I predicted they would. And now I bring you another message—"

In the Scientific Division at Scotland Yard every man was at work with apparatus. Day and night this chance had been awaited. New and more sensitive detectors had been set up in readiness, and now they were operating to the full. As it happened, Forsythe himself was present at the time, his intended journey into space still not made because the dean of Laboratory 9 was still not entirely satisfied with his prowess as a potential space pilot.

"...and that message is that you have four days, no more, to publicly acclaim that you will no longer war with each other, and will instead establish a brotherhood of peace and prosperity. The public declaration of this fact must be followed by visible signs. You have atomic power in two forms—one for destruction and the other for providing energy for everyday uses. I know exactly how many bombs you have in your various stockpiles throughout the world, and I direct that each one of those bombs be fired into outer space inside a guided missile and exploded at a distance far enough away from Earth to cause it no damage. I shall keep a record of the explosions, so do not try and deceive me...."

"Anything?" Forsythe whispered tensely, as one of the engineers delicately adjusted a control.

"Exactly one hundred thousand miles away, chief—and it doesn't vary. But look at that directional indicator there!" Forsythe turned and contemplated an oval-shaped screen. Upon it a spot of intense light was dancing. Behind it, electrically controlled, was a distance meter. Since this latter was linked to a mathematical calculator, it was infallible.... The instrument was a "byproduct" of radar, designed to reflect an energized beam from any object in space that it happened to strike and, once having struck it, to hold it in focus magnetically. By this process, if the object struck were on the move, the fact would be evident upon the moving scale.

"There's something there, traveling at precisely seven thousand miles an hour," Forsythe muttered, his eyes narrowed. "Something a hundred thousand miles away. That raises a question. Why does an interspatial being need to belt along at a speed like that? If anything proves there is no being at all, this does!"

"...and following the destruction of your A and H bombs, you will proceed to destroy everything intended for offense or defense. Your ironclads, your tanks, your jet bombers, all and everything of a harmful nature. One need not fear that one party will jettison his defenses whilst another does not. My order applies to everybody and none can escape it.

"If you do these things, I will give to you the answers to all the problems which beset you—the secrets of space travel, the antidotes for virulent diseases, the mathematical solution to the riddle of Time. I will give you a Paradise on Earth. And if you do *not* do these things? Destruction, my friends! I will scourge your planet from end to end, for only if hostility and bitterness are destroyed can progress flourish.

"Again you will be asking for a sign that I mean

what I say. I ask you to watch the events of the next few days and particularly the behavior of certain men and women whom you all know. They will apparently act of their own free will, as did the financiers, but the real answer will be that I have directed them. Later I shall speak again, and remember what I have told you."

The Conqueror's Voice faded into distance and was gone, but upon the detector screen in the Yard's scientific headquarters that spot of light still danced at a steady rhythm, and the meter readings remained constant.

Forsythe stood thinking. Then: "Only one thing moves in outer space at seven thousand miles an hour, and that's a projectile of some kind. A meteorite is much faster than that. Let me think now: if an unmanned rocket was fired from the Earth and reached far enough out into space, it would retain its initial velocity if it dropped into an orbit of its own. Hell, yes!" he broke off. "Now we're getting somewhere!"

"Meaning," said the technician at the switches, "that somebody fired a projectile into space that retained its initial velocity, and then fell into an orbit which keeps it constantly moving around Earth?"

"That's it," Forsythe nodded. "This projectile is constantly traveling like the ball on the end of a piece of string, held by the parent gravity of Earth."

"It would also account," the technician said, "for the unvarying strength of the radio signal received throughout the world. The distance of the transmitter is constant. In fact, the only thing that now has us guessing is...who is back of it?"

"As to that—" Forsythe reflected somberly. "As to that, I'm no nearer. The Yard has been catching the activities of various scientists and checking up on any who might be missing, but nothing has rung a bell so far. I've been speculating on the idea that there might be somebody aboard this space projectile who is sending the messages, and that's the reason I intend to fly into space and look for myself."

CHAPTER SIX

"I assume," Forsythe asked, looking again at the laboratory technicians, "that there is no clue as to a projectile having taken off? Manned or remote controlled?"

"No clue at all. All possible centers of guided missiles have been interrogated, and there isn't a single projectile that can't be accounted for. Which means that this particular projectile we're looking for must have been built by somebody who knows all the answers about it, and is therefore independent of ordinary scientific sources."

There was silence for a moment, Forsythe considering the floor and the senior technician fiddling idly with switches.

"This unknown quantity definitely has the drop on us," Forsythe confessed presently. "He could have dispatched it—or gone with it—at some time in the night when nobody would be on the alert. In a very short time his exhaust would be beyond visual range and not a soul would be any the wiser."

"Whoever he is, he must be crazy!" the technician declared. "Otherwise he wouldn't want to try and reform the world. He might know he's doomed to failure on that from the very start."

"Don't be too sure!" Forsythe looked up quickly. "Matter of fact, the one thing about this business which I don't like is having to go after a man with such laudable ambition. Heaven knows, if World Brotherhood can be realized—by any logical means—then let it. Yet here am I ordered to find this individual and bring him in like a common criminal because he's broken the law."

"He has, eh? On what charge exactly?"

"Disturbing the peace; spreading gloom and despondency. In short, turning civilization inside out with his threats. That's illegal, and whoever he is he must know that. If I had my own way, I'd let him get away with it, and do nothing. As it is—" Forsythe gave a sigh. "Well, I must keep on trying to sort things out, I suppose."

"I've been thinking—about that Voice. It isn't one that you'd hear any day and think no more about it. It's outstandingly impressive, even hypnotic, in the way it speaks. It seems to me that anybody with a voice like that must be well known. I have been trying to think of a great television, stage, or movie actor who has a voice like that, only I just can't. Why don't you make inquiry of the Dramatic Association and see if they can provide a clue as to who might own the Voice?"

"It's an idea," Forsythe agreed, thinking. "I'm assured by our legal experts that the speaker of the messages is the real culprit who must be arrested, whether his voice is 'live' or only recorded. If somebody is back of him, he'll not come under the law at all. It's like a case of murder. It's the one who actually does the deed who gets landed, not the directive brain behind it. I'm assuming that in this case the owner of the Voice is the guiding brain. I cannot see two people being involved in anything so fantastic as this. Anyhow, I'll take your advice and check up on the Dramatic Association."

Which was exactly what Forsythe did, and as usual he was intensely thorough. He visited not only the headquarters of the Association in London, but also the provincial branches. He listened to endless recordings of excerpts from plays spoken by famous male actors and elocutionists, but nowhere was there a voice that even resembled the rich basso-profundo of the Conqueror.

Meanwhile, comfortable in his new home, Albert waited for signs that the Governments of the world had decided to heed his instructions. But though he heard of hurried secret meetings between heads of State—after which extremely vague statements were issued—there was no visible sign of A or H bombs being projected into space, there to harmlessly explode themselves. As for the jettisoning of small arms like rifles, grenades, revolvers, and suchlike, there was not the remotest evidence.

"It's annoying, Emmy," he confessed to his wife ten days after his second communication. "If the heads of State won't listen, I'm put in the position of having to implement my promise to wipe humanity off the face of the Earth. Obviously I can't do that, nor would I if I could. I'm not the Almighty, when all's said and done."

"Not by any means," Emily agreed lazily, sprawled on the settee in the comfortable lounge. "Whatever you do, Albert, is all right with me. And I'm sorry I misjudged you earlier."

"Because I provided this new home, comforts, and a fair margin of money?" Albert smiled wistfully. "Just a byproduct, Emmy. It's this world problem with which I must get to grips. What can I do now to scare humanity into action?"

He stood thinking, fondling the side of his jaw and gazing out on to the well-kept lawn.

"What can I do to shake these folks into action without harming them?"

"Don't ask me! I'm no scientist—and as a matter of fact I don't think humanity in general is worth all this trouble, especially as all you'll finally get will probably be a kick in the pants."

"Reformers never have an easy road," Albert sighed. "And that is what I am—a reformer, singled out in a modern age to try a super-modern method of maintaining sanity in a rapidly disintegrating social structure. Somehow I must get people to realize that I mean what I say. The case of the four financiers was evidently not pointed enough to implement the issue.... Now let me see: what else is there?"

Long silence. Emily did not exert herself, and there were no disturbances, since the younger children were playing in a room allotted solely to them, and Ethel and Vera were out together for the evening.

"I think," Albert said at last, "that I have it! In the past few weeks I've been near enough to several famous personalities to get their brain frequency readings, and it seems to me that if each one of them acted entirely contrary to normal, it would so startle other famous people—the heads of State, for instance—that they might be inclined to obey the commands I have given."

"What do you propose?" Emily inquired.

"I can't tell you offhand. It depends on what certain celebrated people are noted for, and also which people have provided brain-frequency readings for me. There is one person I can deal with, however, and that is the Minister for International Affairs, Kenneth Cooper. He's known to everybody as an immaculate being who never hurries. What's going to happen if he appears in rags and runs around like a mouse with its tail on fire?"

Emily had little sense of humor, so she did not smile—but Albert did, and very widely. He had suddenly seen the amusing possibilities, wedded to the pious hope that the shock would be great enough to jolt the untouched ones into action.

"The next few days," he said, "are going to show surprising developments. The only trouble is, I cannot give warning beforehand in a message because I haven't recorded it. Indeed, I've only one message left on the tape, and that is the one congratulating the world for having obeyed my commands, and promising that I will keep watch over everybody and only communicate again if there are signs of backsliding."

"Optimistic, aren't you? Recording a message like that before anything has happened?"

"No other way, Emmy. When I fired my projectile into space, fitted with all the necessary remote control gadgets, I knew I'd never be able to recall it, therefore it was essential to plan the messages to fit the possible trend of circumstances. That's another reason why I must make humanity obey, otherwise the last message is useless."

"Thanks for telling me so much. You've never revealed so many facts before."

Albert shrugged. "Can't see it matters now if you do know. I know that for your own good you won't repeat anything—not even to the children. Fact of the matter is, there's a missile circling the Earth, fitted with radio transmitting equipment powered by atomic energy batteries. The atomic energy provides the terrific force which enables my transmission to swamp the normal ones. Naturally, everything is controlled from my workshop and, fortunately for me, there are so many radio wavebands constantly in action, together with radar beams in case of sudden attack from another country, it is quite unlikely for anybody with a detector to single out my remote control radio beam at the infrequent intervals when I use it."

"Use it? What for?"

"To switch on the tape-recording mechanism and radio transmitter. When the equipment is activated, the recorded voice is automatically broadcast in the normal manner, and Earth receivers get the benefit. If there are radio receivers on the Moon, the Selenites will, I imagine, be able to listen too. Radio waves emanate in circles, remember."

"And that's the whole story of what you're up to?"

"Linked with electrical hypnosis, about which you already know, yes."

Emily was silent for a while, studying Albert's thin, eager face. Then:

"It's the Voice itself I can't get over, Albert! Whose is it? Never in a month of Sundays could you make your voice sound like that!"

"No, it's not my voice," Albert smiled. "I told you that long ago."

"Then that means that somebody is in on this with you—and that could be dangerous. I'll never breathe a word, but your partner might."

Albert's smile broadened. "My partner can't. I haven't got one. I'm the only person involved in this business, and I have made myself perfectly safe from the law in case by some unexpected twist I happen to be found out."

"Stop being evasive! That still doesn't explain who is delivering the messages so magnificently."

"Let's call it a Voice, Emmy, and leave it at that. If you were more of a scientist you'd have guessed the truth long ago, particularly if you think back to the nights I used to work such long overtime in the Premier Cinema—"

Emily frowned, and then gradually lost herself in the mists of speculation.

* * * * * * *

Even if the public in general seemed to have relegated the Conqueror's Voice to a back seat, the Press had not. They kept hammering at the subject day after day, demanding to know how far the scientists had progressed in solving the mystery; insisting that some satisfactory answer should be given; as good as ordering that the unrest caused by the "Andromedian" should be brought to a stop before it seriously began to undermine public morale.

To all of which the scientists maintained silence—but Forsythe of the Yard felt it was the signal for him to get more action in the matter. At the end of his resources to track down a famous actor who might be responsible for the Voice, he was left with the only other alternative—to fly out into space and trace the cause of the disturbance, photograph it if need be, or better still steer the projectile—if such it proved to be—back to Earth. So, with the help of the dean of Laboratory 9, he redoubled his efforts to master the final intricacies of piloting a projectile into outer space, and still by special order not a word concerning his activities leaked into the Press.

All the ballyhoo concerning the Conqueror's Voice suited Albert Simpkins to the ground. It kept the business bang in the public eye, which was exactly what he wanted. So, armed with his apparatus, which looked like a portable hurdy-gurdy, he roamed up and down London, electrically hypnotising this and that famous person, giving each one orders which would only be obeyed after twelve hours. This fact gave Albert time to get completely clear so he could enjoy the fun from a distance.

And fun it certainly proved to be! The following day, Kenneth Cooper, the Minister for International affairs, was due to attend the opening ceremony of a new hospital—of which fact Albert Simpkins had been fully aware. The amazement of the populace was therefore complete when the famous Minister, world renowned for his sartorial magnificence, arrived at the hospital in jacket, pants, and shirt which would even have made a tramp look dowdy.

He did not appear in the least disturbed by the sensation he caused, strolling up the red carpet to the entranceway with huge holes in the toecaps of his shoes. Where he had obtained the ragbag he did not even know himself, being under hypnotic compulsion, but he certainly destroyed forever the reputation of immaculacy that he had previously held.

He went through the ceremony perfectly, and the public assumed it was a joke. It was a public that comprised millions, due to the ubiquitous eye of television, therefore the ridicule heaped upon the Minister was absolute. But the newspapers, having long memories, recalled in their evening columns certain words of the Conqueror in which he had suggested that the public should watch, in the coming days, the behavior of certain men and women in the public eye. They would do things contrary to their inclinations, due to the Voice's tremendous hypnotic control—which seemed to indicate that the Minister for International Affairs was not himself.

Had his case been isolated, it would probably not have had great prominence, but he was only one of a dozen of cases, all of which were cited in the evening papers. Gregory Danvers, for instance, the great Shakespearean actor, had staggered a matinee audience by suddenly abandoning *Othello* and behaving like a provincial red-nosed comic, complete with blue jokes. Then there was Claudine del Vilifa, the bustified prima donna straight from Milan who, at a charity performance, had thrown *Aïda* overboard, and instead performed a surprisingly efficient Irish jig!

Apart from Cooper, politicians, apparently, had not come under the mystical influence—purposely, indeed, for Albert wished them to view these other instances and then act out of fear of what might happen to themselves. But artists, actors, actresses, musicians, and the like, had in many ways degraded or otherwise made themselves objects of ridicule. The Press summed it up as a warning—a warning that heads of State must heed. If the Conqueror could so control men and women like this, what might he not do if driven to his threat of destroying the human race if his commands were not obeyed?

The net result, entirely because of public and Press clamor, was for the much-harassed statesmen to call together their colleagues and decide what they must do. Fear! That was the main factor operating now. Fear of being made ridiculous, the one thing no politician—

and particularly an important one—can tolerate.

Hurried consultations with America over the trans-atlantic radio followed the British conferences; and in the eastern half of the world meetings took place in strictest secrecy and arsenals were assessed. These were all happenings which were not reported upon and, in the meantime, the teeming millions of work-aday men and women went about their usual occupa-tions, not sure whether to be frightened or amused by the fact that they were apparently all being studied by a super being from Andromeda.

The "super being" himself, Albert Simpkins, spent his time enjoying the bright weather. Sometimes he hypnotized certain public figures; at others he merely strolled around for the sake of it. On certain occasions Emily accompanied him, finding in the newfound sense of luxury that had descended upon her a certain conviction that Albert was not such a hopeless fool after all. Certainly they would never be in financial difficulty again, and that meant a lot. There was even the possibility, from Emily's point of view, that Albert might suddenly acquire common sense and bring the whole world to obeying him. What one man would do with all the world at his command Emily did not trouble to think—but Albert did, which was why he refrained from the ultimate step.

Meantime, Grant Forsythe was at last proficient in the subtle art of astrophysics. The time had come when he must take the plunge—literally. Midnight of June 27—today—had been selected, and it now lacked five minutes to the zero hour.

He, a few technicians, and the dean of Laboratory 9, were gathered under the misty stars of the proving ground used for the testing of long-range missiles. Nearby stood the specially made one-man projectile that had been designed and converted for Forsythe's especial use. It was loaded with every conceivable necessity—food, weapons, cameras, telescopic and radar devices, air conditioning plant, clothes—everything. Within it there would be just room for Forsythe to lie at full length and operate the controls.

"At this late hour," the dean said, "it seems rather absurd to wonder if your risky flight might not be a waste of time, Mr. Forsythe—but in view of what I have just heard over the radio, I cannot help but have second thoughts."

"Why, what have you heard?" Forsythe's dimly-visible face turned sharply in the twilight as he buttoned up his flying suit.

"America, Britain, and Europe have all agreed to disarm to the limit. A pact to this effect will be signed tomorrow morning by the heads of the three States, and after that the order given by the Voice—to jettison H and A bombs—will be obeyed. Since the Voice has gained his point and brought a vast measure of relief to the world, it seems rather pointless for you to risk your life trying to locate this benefactor."

"Frankly, dean, the whole damned thing's pointless, but it so happens I have a duty to do, and the legal side takes no cognizance of mitigating factors. The issue is that the Voice has transgressed our laws and for that reason must be apprehended, if possible, and brought before an international court to explain himself. I know it's absurd—fantastic—but the law has never been anything else."

"Zero approaching, Mr. Forsythe," a technician warned, and at that the pugnacious Yard man turned quickly, shook hands with those around him and then squeezed himself into the narrow confines of the projectile's cabin. The airlock slammed and, within, Forsythe swung over the clamps, which also activated the pilot light.

For a second or two he lay collecting himself and sweating freely under the intensity of the moment; then his hand reached to the controls. Instantly the massively powerful rocket engines at the rear blasted forth, and the small craft began to rise swiftly from the ramp.

Forsythe was lying prone, enduring now the tortures of the damned that he had undergone in artificial conditions in Laboratory 9: the crushing pressures, the labouring under 5, 10, 15, 20 atmospheres; the tearing strain which felt as though it would smash his heart and rip the flesh from his bones. And down below, the swirling bowl of lights which was Earth, merging at length into a titanic green crescent where the sunlight was bringing the dawn.

Faint, fighting for breath, the Yard man hung on, knowing from experience in the "conditioning chamber" just how long this mortal anguish would last. Then the projectile flashed through the last limits of the atmospheric envelope and into free space. Automatically the rockets cut out and the machine instantly lost all sense of weight. From feeling as though he were being squeezed into the padded floor beneath a hydraulic press, Forsythe now was as light as a feather, dizzy with the sudden return of exuberant circulation.

Tough though he was, and trained through the weeks to this supreme test of man's endurance, it took him a full fifteen minutes to feel something like his normal self. Then he turned his attention to the narrow outlook port directly in front of him and gazed upon the depthless, unthinkable majesty of space. Its fascination held him in thrall. Everything was just as he had pictured it would be.

A blinding sun girdled by prominences and backed by the pearly grandeur of the corona; an argent, three-quarter moon, its edge hacked out against the ebony backdrop of infinity—and then the stars—depthless diamonds, unmisted and searing in their brilliance, stretching as far as vision could reach, and then untold light-centuries beyond that again. The sweep and glory of infinity was something that Forsythe's intensely materialistic soul could not possibly assimilate.

Then abruptly he was back on the job, remembering his purpose. He had to travel 100,000 miles, practically halfway to the Moon, in his endeavour to locate his objective. That, at his present speed, was quite a fair distance, since the projectile, being of the slimmest and smallest proportions, had not had the terrific escape velocity destined for the big exploratory space-ships in an age yet to come.

Forsythe settled himself as well as he could, rehearsing movements which he had gone over time and again, and which finally gave him the maximum bodily comfort in the minimum of space.... So he flew onwards, listening part of the time to radio news from Earth, most of which was concerned with the sensa-tional decision of the world's dominant powers to jettison their major weapons of war. The rest of the time he kept a watch on his instruments, particularly the radar beam, the deflection of which would show if it hit a solid object—other than the distant Moon—anywhere ahead. To differentiate between the Moon and any other object was simple enough. All he had to do was keep the directive beam diagonal to the Moon so it could not possibly impinge against it.

On and on, on his incredibly fantastic mission. He slept, he ate, he stared into unending space, he lay musing on the mysteries of life and death; he watched the instruments, listened to the radio, wondered if he would meet with success. And then, after seemingly endless hours, there came that deflection of the radar beam detector for which he had been waiting.

To the northwest his forward motion—the space being divided into compass points on the cosmic map beside him—something had momentarily "echoed" from the radar thrust. Almost instantly it was gone again, but this did not bother Forsythe. If the object was moving at 7,000 miles an hour, as had been calculated back on Earth, it would take a fixed period to circumnavigate the orbit round the Earth and would then return to the same position and again cross the radar beam at a nearer point since, in the interval, the projectile would have advanced further on its journey.

Which, to Forsythe's jubilation, was exactly what happened. At the appointed time he beheld an object that was obviously a long-range missile traveling at high velocity, glinting in the sunlight. In silence he studied its soundless rush through infinity, and at the same time the automatic movie cameras photographed it. But this was not enough for Forsythe: he had to know everything there was to know concerning it, so very carefully he manoeuvred his projectile towards the orbit which the missile was taking, according to the automatic trackers anyhow.

Once he had reached the fringe of this orbit Forsythe turned his machine slightly so it was parallel with the orbit.

Then he began to cruise at something like 6,000 miles an hour. By this method, he figured, he would eventually be overtaken by the missile. He could then accelerate until he was keeping pace with it. After that, actual boarding of the missile might be possible. Having come this far Forsythe was prepared to risk death itself to find an answer to the mystery.

Sure enough, right on the precalculated time, the missile finally began to reappear in the void, having completed its circuit of the nearby looming Earth.

Forsythe laid his hands on the controls, ready for action, watching tensely as the fast-moving missile swept nearer. It seemed only a matter of moments before it was level, and by this time Forsythe had himself built up enough acceleration to keep pace with the missile—and in this wise he was able to study it. There was no chance now of him getting "out of step" with the missile, since they were both traveling free space at the same trajectory and their two gravities were interlocked.

So Forsythe lay contemplating the missile, noting its construction and the obvious lack of skill that had gone into the making of the thing. It was spaceworthy enough—no doubt of that—but the little touches which a skilled engineer would have added were absent, which to Forsythe indicated that a trained scientist was not back of the project. The only answer was a clever amateur.

Finally Forsythe reached his hand to the radio switch, and within a few moments he had contacted Earth. It was the voice of the dean of Laboratory 9 that answered him.

"I've located the source of the mystery, dean," Forsythe said, "and I'm relying on you to take the news back to Scotland Yard. You can tell the world that it isn't a man from Andromeda—or anything resembling it! It's a very homemade missile, a rough-and-ready version of the interplanetary rockets now being perfected. At the moment I'm keeping pace with it as it pursues its seven-thousand-mile-an-hour orbit round

Earth. My next move will be to examine it, and I'll report again after that.... Any fresh news from Earth which I ought to know about?"

Brief pause whilst the radio wave hurtled back and forth over the void. "Nothing vital, Forsythe, except that I still think all this is a waste of time. General disarmament seems to be everywhere, and it seems to me that if we tell the world that disarmament has been obtained by a hoax, it will have a disastrous effect. Can't you soft-pedal things a little?"

"Sorry," Forsythe replied bluntly. "I've been given an assignment and I mean to complete it. I've just got to! Be more than my job's worth to fall down on the case now."

"As you wish." The dean gave a disappointed sigh.

Forsythe, satisfied that everything he was doing was right in the line of duty, no matter what his personal reactions, eased his body up to the limit and then drew forth a spacesuit from the nearby locker. Here again he had to rely on the training he had undergone in order to "pour" himself into the heavy mass of rubber, metal-mesh, and plastic. It took him several minutes; then he checked over his instruments and particularly his gun—for he did not know but what hostile intelligent life might be within the nearby missile. This done, he switched off the air supply and pulled across the bar of the escape hatch.

That which followed was very similar to a high altitude parachute jump, only far more hair-raising. The air pressure within the control room, still level at fourteen pounds to the square inch even though further supply had been cut off, blasted out into space and flung Forsythe with it. Helplessly he was impelled into the void, turning crazy somersaults in the process and having nothing around him except endless depth. He could not, of course, fall to destruction, since there was neither up nor down in the accepted sense. But what he could and did do was collide with the nearby missile and remain anchored to it by reason of its slight but appreciable mass.

Dazed, he struggled up the projectile's metal plates until he had reached the summit—a narrow deck like that upon a submarine. From here, feeling transiently godlike, he surveyed all infinity, then his own projectile nearby with its open hatch, and lastly, the titanic globe of Earth 100,000 miles away. He could descry clouds, continents, oceans—then just in time he turned his gaze away as an overwhelming dizziness sought to overpower him.

Mastering himself, he crept along the missile's deck until he came to what he knew must be the entrance panel. That it was locked on the outside satisfied him that there was nobody within. Whoever had fired this missile into space had sealed it from the exterior.

With an electric cutter, operated from the batteries on his back, Forsythe cut the metal hasp through and raised the heavy lid. No air came gushing upwards to bowl him off into space again, which once more was evidence of the absence of life within the vessel. Still with his gun ready, just in case, Forsythe crept into the entrance hole and gained the missile's gloomy interior. It was so small in here, and so cramped with instruments, that the Yard man could hardly move, particularly as he too was bloated above normal size by his spacesuit. He tugged his torch from his belt and flashed the beam around him, studied with intent interest the mass of radio instrument complication on every hand. He recognised high-power transmitting apparatus, and to it was linked an obvious remote-control system. The curious thing was that everything looked so utterly homemade. One part of the paneling, for instance, had been fastened down with an ordinary timber nail instead of a chromium-plated screw. The stamp of the amateur was everywhere.

"Yet, what an amateur!" Forsythe whispered in admiration inside his helmet. "If I could think up stuff like this, I certainly would not be a wolfhound for Scotland Yard."

He regretted privately that his scientific knowledge was not greater, for here was a wealth of scientific accomplishment, much of which escaped him. Apart from the radio transmitting equipment, he also recognised a sound projector, differently constructed from a sound-film projector in that it ran a soundtrack only, and no visual.

Forsythe stooped towards this contrivance, noted it was linked by multi-colored wires to the remote-control devices, and then took his microcamera from his pocket to photograph the essential parts. Before he could achieve focus, however, he found himself suddenly rocked violently by an explosion or vibration from outside.

Explosion? Out here in space? He had felt it, but not heard it, which was in conformity with the vacuum of the void. Puzzled, he put his microcamera back in his spacesuit pocket and lumbered to the opening through which he had entered. Poking his helmeted head into space he surveyed wonderingly—

And that was as far as he got. At that very moment something no more than a dozen yards over his head burst with cataclysmic violence. For an instant space was drenched with unholy brightness which drowned even the searing glare of the sun. There was no sound, but there was a downpouring of radiation and a tremendous pressure wave.

Forsythe reeled back into the missile's instrument room, his skull torn with blinding pain. Sight and hearing had been destroyed in those few seconds. He was only a shell of a man, life deserting him in the half minute that ensued. He did not even detect the further frightful explosions that burst around him, even though his dying body registered their shock. Such was the radiation they generated, it pierced right through the insulation of his spacesuit, but did not affect the missile in which he lay even though it rocked under the soundless impacts.

Forsythe died without knowing what had destroyed him. Yet the explanation was simple enough. From Earth, A and H bombs which nations had had stored up were being fired into space, there to explode. Since

Forsythe's journey into the void had been secret, nobody could ever have thought that a man might be out there, directly in the line of fire!

CHAPTER SEVEN

No man—except the dean of Laboratory 9—guessed the tragic truth when frantic radio calls to Forsythe met with no response, and the truth was further confirmed when astronomers, watching the exploding atomic bombs in space, announced finally that all of them had been successfully jettisoned at 100,000 miles distance.

"This," the dean said to those few scientists and technicians who knew of Forsythe's venture, "is nothing less than damnable. Forsythe was on the verge of discovering the truth about the Conqueror's Voice, yet now he must be assumed dead. There are two answers to the matter. Either one of us makes a second trip into the void, to piece together the story which Forsythe half told me, or we keep quiet and allow the Conqueror to have his way. Of the two alternatives I prefer the latter. The Conqueror—who must undoubtedly be somebody on Earth here—has by his very audacity ushered in a new era of peace and goodwill. I would prefer to let it go at that."

Unfortunately, however, the dean was only a lone voice crying in the wilderness. There was no doubt that his view was the only sane one, but there were other factors to be reckoned with—Scotland Yard, for one. The Scientific Branch naturally knew of the assignment into space that Forsythe had taken, and when no word came from him, the Assistant Commissioner for the Scientific Division bluntly wanted to know why. And to him the venerable dean of Laboratory 9 was obliged to give the facts.

"So he got that far, then?" the A.C. asked slowly when the story had been told. "He had definitely proved that a guided missile of very homemade variety is back of the Conqueror's Voice?"

"So he told me. He could have been mistaken, I suppose."

The A.C. shook his head. "Not Forsythe, dean. He was one of the best men in the Division, and certainly one of the most courageous. He saw a missile all right, and that means that the population of this planet have been hoaxed by an amateur scientist pretending to be a super-being from Andromeda. The law says that sort of thing can't be permitted."

"Oh, damn the law, Commissioner! Look at the good this Unknown has done—and may yet do. What kind of fools would we be to try and locate him, stop him, and maybe imprison him?"

"The law," the A.C. stated deliberately, "has to be upheld. If we ignore it in this instance, we must in others, and that way lies chaos. We know now, once and for all, that we are looking for an idealistic scientist with more than his share of ingenuity. He has got to be found! Don't you realize that he may not always remain beneficent? Even the mildest man, if he finds himself suddenly gifted with supreme powers, can lose his head. So might this individual. It is not only his sending of a mystery missile into space that is illegal, but also his tampering with the personalities of famous people. I don't have to remind you of the behavior of certain folk recently, do I?"

"I must admit that I had forgotten that," the dean confessed.

"The law says that the liberty of the individual must not be interfered with in any way, yet here we have this unknown doing exactly as he likes. Whether his work be beneficial or otherwise, he is still acting illegally and we intend to leave nothing unturned to discover who he is."

The dean was silent, absently studying the desk before him.

"There are also other significant pressures being brought to bear upon me and my department," the A.C. added presently, and at that the dean looked up in surprise.

"I'm referring to Big Business. Under that generalisation I include armament kings, financiers, and others who stand to lose much of their fortunes through the world's decision to disarm. None of them like this disarmament for obvious reasons, and they keep thrusting it down my throat that the whole thing is ill-conceived and dangerous and probably a very clever trick on the part of our international enemies. Because I have no real facts to the contrary, I can't deny the assumption.

So you see, dean, I have to carry on with the investigation. I shall put Douglas Marshall in charge of it in Forsythe's place. He's a good man, but he'll never be a Forsythe."

There was nothing more the dean could do, and he realized it. He departed a few moments later, quite resolved in his own mind that there should be no second trip into space in an effort to discover the Unknown's secrets. The dean had reached that age of maturity where he could appreciate that peace—by whatever means it was attained—was wholly desirable, and he was resolved not to raise a finger to disturb it.

And Albert Simpkins? He was a perfectly happy man because the world had obeyed his request. Since the story of Forsythe's venture into space had been suppressed, Albert was not aware of how close he had come to having his whole remote control set-up exposed. Nor was he aware that a certain quarter of the scientific world knew full well that a "box of tricks" was behind the Conqueror's Voice, and that his missile had been scientifically located. He still fondly believed that the illusion of a being from Andromeda was accepted throughout the world, and he reveled in the sensation thereby produced.

"Indeed," he told Emily one evening, "there are no limits to what can be done from here on."

Emily was surprised, and looked it. "But I thought you'd be satisfied with disarmament? Having put the world at peace what more is there to accomplish?"

"What more! Did I not promise the world the antidotes for malignant diseases, all the benefits of science? And you ask what more!"

"But you can't give those things, Albert!" Emily insisted. "You are a perfectly ordinary man, though I'll admit you are much more of a scientific genius than I had ever imagined, but you just can't give anybody the answer to deadly diseases, and all the rest of it."

"I can—and I shall."

"But how?"

"By the same way in which I gave other people powers they don't normally possess. I gave Vera a flawless soprano voice, didn't I, for a brief while? How do you imagine I did that?"

"Electrical hypnosis, wasn't it?"

"Only partly. You see," Albert continued, seating himself close beside Emily, "the hypnosis part is only the medium in between. It is the process by which the person under the influence is compelled to submerge his or her individual will. If we accept the unalterable factor that the mind is master of the body—which it certainly is—it is quite enough for the person under hypnosis to be compelled to believe that he or she can accomplish a certain thing. It is the belief that does it, and the body responds automatically. Convince a man he can sing superbly—and I mean convince him, which is only possible by amplified hypnosis—and he will sing superbly. It is as simple as that. That is what I did to Vera. Of course, the moment the hypnosis is removed, the conferred ability is lost. That, though, is no detriment. I can keep the power on long enough for the person to 'discover' his or her great gift and give it to the world. Once it has been given and understood by others, it does not matter if the original conceiver of it has forgotten how he or she did it."

"Oh!" Emily said, and waited stolidly for the next.

"I could demonstrate it quite easily, Emmy, by making you believe you are the world's greatest artist. Under that influence you would paint masterpieces greater than any by Leonardo de Vinci."

"Wouldn't get me very far, though, would it?" Emily sighed. "In any case, Albert, I'll take your word for it, and in a vague sort of way I can see what you're driving at. You mean, don't you, that if you forced a famous medical man to believe that he had the cure for, say, consumption, he really would find it and hand it on to the medical fraternity?"

"Exactly. I myself know of no such cure, and neither would the doctor concerned—but by the insistent mental assertion, through amplified hypnosis, that he does know the answer for consumption, he would inevitably find it because he would believe he could."

Albert got to his feet, an ecstatic look in his eyes. He began to move restlessly about the big lounge.

"This opens up a colossal field, Emily! It is using the mysterious power of mind to such a wonderful purpose! Nowhere, I swear, will I ever use this hypnotic power for evil motives. I intend only to benefit the human race."

"That," Emily pointed out, "is quite a turnabout. When you first started all this monkey business, you said you were doing it so you could feel what it was like to have the whole world obeying you after it had called you a fool for so long. Now you talk about helping all and sundry."

"Yes, in all honesty I do." Albert's small, uninteresting face was deadly serious. "You cannot realize what it is like, Emmy, to know you have supreme power to make or break the human race. It makes you understand that the opportunity is not given just for the satisfying of personal grievances. It is given so it can be used wisely—and that is exactly what I am trying to do with it. By degrees I am trying to discover the main ills that beset mankind, then I shall electrically hypnotize those public figures best fitted to deal with scientific problems and compel them to find the answers. That, I say, can usher in the Golden Age."

The door of the lounge clicked as Vera came in. She was in tennis outfit, racquet in hand and a blazer over her arm. For some reason she was looking deathly pale, and upon the side of her forehead was a monstrous blue-black bruise.

"What on earth—!" her mother exclaimed, struggling to her feet. "What happened to you, Vee?

Vera did not answer. She moved unsteadily to the settee and sat heavily upon it, resting her head on her hand. Albert gave her a puzzled glance, and then opened the French windows a little wider to the soft summer evening breeze.

"I recall," Vera continued, gently fingering "I—I got hit with a tennis ball," Vera explained at last, looking up. "It half stunned me for a moment anyway. I didn't feel up to playing any more so I came home. I'd be glad of a drink, please."

Albert provided it—neat brandy. The girl coughed over it, but the color began to return to her cheeks.

"What was Hal thinking of that he didn't bring you home?" Albert demanded, and at that Vera smiled rather bitterly.

"We had a bit of a tiff, dad. He seemed to get the idea that I was making a lot of fuss over nothing. He said the tennis ball couldn't possibly have hit me so hard as to knock me silly. Been a different matter if it had been a cricket ball."

"You should know, love," her mother said anxiously.

Vera handed the glass up to her father, her eyes thoughtful.

"Hal may have been right," she said slowly. "It wasn't so much the blow of the ball that knocked me out as a sudden awful pain in the head. It was only brief, but it half killed me! I don't know what it was, but when it had gone, I sort of felt that something had happened to my mind. I found myself remembering such a lot of things that I'd completely forgotten."

Albert, who had reached the french windows in order to return Vera's empty glass to the cocktail cabinet, turned slowly and looked at her. She looked at him in return. They could have been strangers on the very worst of terms. There was not the least trace of father and daughter affection between them.

"Now what's wrong?" Emily demanded, glancing

from one to the other. "What are you looking at your dad like that for, Vee?"

Vera did not answer. Instead she got slowly to her feet, steadied herself, then went across to where her father was standing. He watched her fixedly as she approached him.

"Dad, when I got that pain in the head I remembered something very special," she said deliberately. "I remembered being in your workshop-laboratory— that place we used to have before we came here. I remembered you were going to teach me how to play a concerto or something...I remembered everything! Your radio machinery, your electrical compulsion— the whole fantastic set-up!"

"So?" Albert Simpkins' voice was deadly quiet.

"I recall," Vera continued, gently fingering the bruise on her forehead, "that I was going to tell the police all I knew about your activities, not only because they'd offered fifty thousand pounds reward, but chiefly because I felt you were not being fair in controlling people against their will. Then I forgot all about everything—until tonight when that tennis ball hit me."

Emily drifted forward, her eyes frightened. Albert looked at his daughter's determined face, then at the swelling bruise on her forehead.

"You'd better fix that bruise," he said. "Your mother will help you."

"The bruise can wait, dad. It's better now than it was. And don't try and evade the issue, either!"

Albert's eyes hardened. "How dare you speak to me

like that! You should be ashamed of yourself!"

"So should you! It wasn't enough that I was the unwilling guinea pig the first time when you made me act the fool on the kitchen table! You had to do it again! And you had the impudence to try and destroy my memory so I couldn't say a thing about your activities! You'll never know how much I tried to puzzle things out for myself, how I tried to reconcile my mysterious collapse in the workshop just as you were going to show me how I could play a concerto. For the life of me I couldn't fathom why the details of the whole thing kept eluding me. Tonight, though, I found the answer."

"Apparently," Albert said, musing, "the blow on the head produced enough shock to disturb the electrical dormancy I had placed upon certain cells of your brain. It is similar to a blind man suddenly seeing under the influence of a shock, or of a deaf person recovering hearing following a sharp and unexpected blow. Mental, all of it."

Vera was silent, her mouth bitter and her eyes hard.

"About your bruise, love," her mother ventured. "Sooner you get it fixed the—"

"Let me alone, mum! I haven't finished yet. Dad, I'm entitled to know why you took such liberties with me."

"I took no liberties, Vee. On that evening you were in a particular irascible mood, just as you are now, and at that time it did not suit my purpose that in a moment of impetuosity you should go to the police and upset all my plans. So I blanked out your memory on that particular incident. It did you no harm and as it has since been proved, it enabled me to do a great deal of good."

"Never for a moment did you consult my wishes!" Vera cried hotly. "You calmly stand there and say you blanked out part of my memory because I didn't happen to act as you thought I should! What do you think I am? A laboratory specimen?"

"That's ridiculous, Vee, and you know it."

"I don't know it! You bend everything to your scientific experiments, including me. And I resent it! I resent it all the more when I think of the implacable way in which you do it!"

"Since then," Albert said, his voice still deliberate, "many things have happened to prove my way of thinking to be right. I have brought peace to the world. I have—"

"You've made many famous people look ridiculous too! You have made me look ridiculous even when I'm your own daughter! What right have you to go around meddling in people's lives and changing their ways of thought? What right?"

"As to a right, none at all," Albert shrugged. "Everything has been a means to an end. That end has partly been achieved, and if you were half as loyal to me as you ought to be, it would make the job much simpler!"

"I'd have been much more loyal to you if you'd taken me into your confidence instead of treating me like a child. I discovered your whole Conqueror's Voice secret long ago, dad, and you knew I had. Rather than admit everything to me, you tried to blot out my knowledge of it. That I can never forgive."

A retort almost came from Albert's lips, but he had no chance to utter it, for Vera turned away angrily, swayed a little at the abrupt swing she gave herself, and then headed from the room, snatching up her blazer and racquet on the way. Emily put her hands together indecisively, looked at her husband, then at last fled after her daughter. Albert turned as the door closed and threw himself into the armchair.

"Damn!" he swore, and compressed his lips.

Half an hour later Emily returned into the lounge, her face troubled. Albert, still in the armchair in the gathering twilight, gave her a questioning glance.

"Well, Emmy, has she cooled off?"

"'Fraid not. Now she's got over the bump on the head, she's angrier than ever. She'll be bound to force her opinions on Ethel, Dick, and Betty when they come in, and that'll mean a lovely household!"

"Just like old times," Albert said dryly, and Emily gave him a hurt look.

"I've tried to improve, Albert, since I've seen what you can do. You know I have! I don't slang you like I used to."

"Only because you're afraid of what I'll do to you if you do. Believe me, Emmy, I know you so well—"

Albert glanced up as the youngest members of the family, Dick and Betty, came in together. They were smudged and untidy from a happy evening in the fields.

"Listen, you two," Albert told them curtly. "You'll

find Vee upstairs in her room and she'll probably tell you a lot of things about me. You are not to listen to her! Understand? You are not to listen! Not a word of it is true."

Brother and sister looked at each other quite at a loss, and for this reason they gave no promises. Emily took them in hand, and once again Albert was left alone. Presently he heard sounds overhead as the children were put to bed; then Ethel came in through the French windows—long-legged Ethel, still a happy schoolgirl and probably the only one who really loved her father and her home.

"'Lo, dad...." She came forward as he sat thinking in the dying light. "Where's mum? I want my supper. I'm hungry."

"Be a miracle if you were not," Albert told her. "Here—sit down a moment. I want to ask you something."

Ethel obeyed, perching on the thick arm of the easy chair.

"You are old enough, Ethel, to have a pretty good idea of what is going on in the world. For instance, you're old enough to know about the Conqueror's Voice."

Ethel laughed. "You bet I am! You do it wonderfully well, dad. I never knew you were a ventriloquist."

"You mean—" Albert stared at her. "You mean you know that I—"

"I don't know anything for certain because you've never said anything. That's all right, I suppose, since you're the boss. But that workshop-laboratory you keep locked up, the fact that you have retired, the money we've suddenly got, and the way you always seem to know when the Voice is going to speak, is quite enough for me. Besides, you've dropped an awful lot of hints, you know, and I've sort of tied two and two together. You are the Voice, aren't you?" Ethel asked blandly.

"No, dear, I am not the Voice. My voice could never sound like that."

"It might by scientific means. I'm top in physics at school, don't forget. Maybe I get it from you."

"Maybe," her father muttered. "Fact remains, I am not the Voice. If the law ever catches up on me, they can't accuse me of being the Voice."

"But why should the law catch up? Look what wonderful things have happened since the Voice spoke! Everybody ought to be grateful, that's what I say. I have quite a wonderful daddy, and it's hard not to say so sometimes to those chumps at school."

"Listen to me, Ethel." Albert put his hand firmly on her wrist. "Your sister Vee is, I think, going to cause trouble. She'll do what she can to blacken me in your eyes, chiefly because I once made her a part of my scientific experiments without her consent. If she does that—"

"I'll knock her for six," Ethel interrupted cheerfully. "Vee's an ass sometimes, dad. Gets highbrow ideas. I'll settle her, and quick, because nothing you do can ever be wrong to me. Now where's mum? I'll die of starvation if I don't find her."

Albert smiled faintly to himself as she went through the gloom of the lounge and disappeared. He sat back in his chair and looked at the gathered stars. In his mind's eye he pictured his missile racing on its eternal seven-thousand-mile-an-hour journey round the Earth. Only one more message was needed, the one already recorded, congratulating the world on its common-sense in heeding his instructions.

And Vera? Albert's thoughts clouded as he thought of her, the one unmanageable one of the family. She was by no means a bad girl, but she was certainly intensely individual, with the queerest personal likes and dislikes. She could be a definite danger. Albert closed his eyes and pondered. At least, he had intended to ponder, but instead he found himself staring at a great yawning abyss of space in which there lay the mighty Nebula of Andromeda. A curious sensation stole over him as he sat there, a feeling that he was somehow being trans-ported through infinity— No, not being transported. That was hardly it. It was more as though a part of his mind were being sucked dry. Something was draining out of his consciousness, something connected with that huge Andromeda Nebula. It was almost as though paralysis gripped him as he fought to open his eyes and break the queer sensation gripping him.

"Asleep, Albert?" That did it. The voice of Emily, matter-of-fact as ever, broke the spell. Albert opened his eyes and blinked.

"Sorry," he apologized. "I dropped off, I'm afraid. Just started dreaming.... How's Vee going on? Did

Ethel get her supper?"

"Get it?" Emily repeated, surprised. "She's been in bed an hour. I've been here quite some time, but I didn't disturb you. I heard you muttering something, so I thought I'd wake you up."

Emily sat down nearby and added: "I've listened upstairs, but I can't hear any talking. Apparently Vee's asleep and probably Ethel is too by now. Dick and Betty dropped off long ago in their own room. But it doesn't make the problem any simpler, Albert. What are we going to do if Vee doesn't have a change of heart?"

"I don't quite know," Albert replied, musing. "It is possible, of course, that the police are no longer interested in the Voice, since everything—or nearly everything—the Voice set out to accomplish has proved successful. Only fools would try and break down the peace that has been forced upon the world. I understand that the next move of the Governments, now all the A and H bombs have been exploded, is to be the sinking of warships, destruction of warplanes, and so forth. I really cannot think that one girl—if Vee went that far—could do much damage. It is something I have to risk."

"And if things don't work out as you expect and the police come investigating? What then?"

"I shan't run away," Albert replied quietly. "Of that you can be sure. I haven't done anything to be ashamed of. Rather the contrary in fact."

Emily did not pursue the topic any further, but she was certainly extremely uneasy.

She knew Vera's erratic and impetuous temperament, and her ability to nurture a fancied wrong until it was out of all proportion in her mind.

Next morning, however, she did not refer to the matter at all during breakfast; but on the other hand she was not particularly talkative either.

Albert, for his part, had his own plans for the day. There were two famous medical men he had to contact—unknown to them—and he hoped that the outcome of the contact would mean their acquiring sudden and remarkable knowledge of how to cure certain dangerous illnesses. So, in the bright summer morning, Albert presently sallied forth, his "box of tricks" slung over his shoulder as usual.

He did not return for lunch—to Emily's surprise—but towards mid-afternoon he rang up.

"I'm in the thick of it, Emmy," came his voice over the wire. "For obvious reasons I can't say too much, but you remember my saying last night that once the influence was turned on, I must hold it until the effect is achieved?"

"I remember. What about it?"

"Well, that's how things are now. I don't know when I'll be back. Expect me when you see me. Incidentally, did Vee say anything further at lunch?"

"No, but her temper didn't seem to be improved from breakfast time. It seems she met Hal on the way home to lunch and he's broken with her, or something. All over that tennis ball and the fuss she made over an apparently trivial injury. Looks to me like Vee's unlucky day."

"There are better boys than Hal in the world," Albert said calmly. "Bye for now, Emmy. See you later."

Albert emerged from the telephone kiosk determined to give to the World—via two medical men—the solutions to two of the world's most malignant diseases.

CHAPTER EIGHT

In another quarter of the town Vera Simpkins was doing her work badly and getting into hot water in consequence. The reason for her inattention to business was not far to seek: she was so disturbed in mind, partly over her father and partly over her break with Hal, her fiancé, that she could not concentrate properly. There was, though, yet another reason for her abnormal behavior. The reaction upon her mentality following the sudden return of a lost portion of her memory, had produced a decidedly nervous condition. Today the physical side was responding unpleasantly to the tempestuous events of the previous night.

All things considered, Vera was in a decidedly bad temper when she left her place of business that evening, and it was this state of mind, more than anything else, which was now impelling her actions. She would inform the police of her father's activities. At least it would mean that he would never again try and enforce his will upon those who were not prepared to accept it.

This in mind, Vera walked the hot streets of London with decisive tread, but before she was halfway to her destination, she commenced to feel all the signs of exhaustion. A most unusual thing for her, for she usually reveled in hot weather. Definitely she was out of sorts—limp, irritable, and feeling extremely dizzy. She paused close beside one of the small parks that abounded in the city center and turned into it, finding a quiet spot beside the lake. She found herself vaguely wondering why she had come here at all—just like some old woman who could not walk a few yards without feeling fit to drop.

Everywhere was quiet. Most people were at tea. The tranquility of the evening would find the throngs strolling. Vera was glad of the silent calm. It soothed her strangely outraged nerves, even if it did not cause her to change her mind about her father. Deep down, she had the idea that she was going to do the community a service by exposing her father's extraordinary scientific powers: this, be it said in justice to her, was her main conviction. That she was actually acting spitefully—or intended to—never occurred to her.

As she thus sat, pondering, she watched with interest the curious bright light that had mysteriously formed over the nearby lake. Absently she noticed that the swans were speeding away from it as fast as they could go.

A bright light? Vera studied it with awakened interest as it appeared to grow larger. It certainly could not be from the sun because the trees formed dense shadows. Perhaps, then, it was some kind of electrical phenomenon produced by the heat and forming at this spot because water is an excellent conductor of electricity.

Perhaps it—

Vera got suddenly to her feet in alarmed amazement for the bright light had become so intense it hurt her eyes to look upon it. Also, it was now spinning violently and generating a weird cramping static. Abruptly it flashed away from the water and over the pathway to where Vera stood in paralyzed wonder, peering through half-closed eyes.

Utterly silent, yet blasting forth an energy that sucked every scrap of strength from Vera's body, the phenomenon kept on coming straight for her. She fell limply, for the simple reason that her legs could not sustain her weight. She lay like a rag doll, arms flung wide, her handbag on the sloping grass verge, her face to the shale-covered pathway. And the spinning top of light still traveled—but now it went upwards and at length melted altogether. The evening was quiet again, and Vera lay exactly as she had fallen.

Until a park ranger, on the perpetual lookout for forbidden practices in the park area, came upon her. He stared in wonder for a moment and then went down on his knees beside her. His amazement was complete when he noticed that her hair was severely singed and that there were burns down one side of her face and across her eyes. Her clothes, too, as he held on to her, crumbled in his hands as though rotten with age. Here was the strangest thing the ranger, or anybody else for that matter, had ever encountered.

Unavoidably the ranger gathered a wondering crowd around him as he carried the body to his headquarters in the center of the recreation ground. By the time he had finished the trip, the girl's clothes had practically rotted to shreds. All he could do was place her on a long board supported on trestles, cover her with a tarpaulin and then grab the phone to summon the police. And since it had all happened in the Metropolitan Area it was Scotland Yard who responded to his call.

"It's the queerest thing I've ever seen," the ranger told the square-jawed inspector when he arrived. "There she was, burned as you see her now, and her clothes falling to bits as though acid had rotted them."

The inspector nodded, but he did not say anything. Beside him, a detective-sergeant made notes. A police surgeon was busy at the moment, examining the corpse and looking vaguely puzzled at the same time. Finally he replaced the tarpaulin over the burned face and looked up.

"Been dead about thirty minutes," he announced. "The cause of death isn't clear until I've made a post-mortem. I would say, from this preliminary examination, that she died from severe electric shock which caused heart failure."

"Similar to somebody being struck by lightning?" the inspector suggested, pondering.

"Very similar, yes. I've seen cases like this before when electricity has done its worst. The poor kid certainly got a packet from somewhere."

Having done all he could for the moment, the surgeon packed up his bag and hurried out. The inspector moved, looked under the tarpaulin for a while, then replaced it. His sharp gray eyes turned to the ranger.

"Any identification? Anything to guide us as to her identity or address?"

"I found her handbag on the grass verge when I had the place searched afterwards. Here it is."

The inspector took it, tipping the contents onto the little table nearby. Finally he picked up a bus contract.

"Mmmm.... Vera Patricia Simpkins, The Rollins, Medway Crescent, West Central. That's a help, anyway. Be a shock to her folks, too, if she has any. Sergeant, you'd better be on your way and break the bad news. I'll carry on here."

"Right, sir."

And, some half hour ahead of the sergeant, Albert Simpkins returned home. He put his "box of tricks" in the laboratory-workshop and locked up the place as usual. Then he came into the lounge through the open French windows. As usual, Emily was lounging in the armchair, reading a romantic novel—but she put it down as Albert came in.

"Altogether," he said, "I think we might call that a good day's work! I managed to get things finished off sooner than I'd expected, so maybe I'm in time for the evening dinner?"

"We can start any moment you like," Emily responded. "I have only got to give the word to the domestics. Vera isn't in yet—if we're going to wait for her?"

Albert glanced in some surprise towards the clock. "*Late,* isn't she? Usually comes in for dinner even if she is going out for the evening."

"*Usually,* yes. My fear is that perhaps she's delayed herself by going to the police. I just can't rid myself of the idea that that intention was in her mind."

"We'll cross that bridge when we come to it, Emmy." Albert seated himself and relaxed. "We can wait a few minutes longer, anyhow, whilst I tell you what I've done. I've fixed Sir Mortimer Cartwright and Dr. Gerald Maxford so that they will hand to the world the antidotes for tuberculosis and arthritis in a reasonably short space of time. I worked first on one and then on the other. The reaction instruments on my equipment showed that the mental compulsion wave I generated at them was fully absorbed. That means they will find the solution I have willed them to find—not because I know what it is, but because I have compelled them to believe that *they* know what it is. It is all a matter of belief. They'll find the answers all right: the well of intelligent conception is bottomless."

"That way," Emily said absently, "one could almost find anything by simply believing it can be done."

"Why not? Nothing is impossible to mind. It is the material set-up that sets the limits. The hardest part was holding the men under the influence for a long spell of time. I had to be sure they were within range and would not move out of it.... Fortunately, I had a fine day, a reasonably close recreation ground in proximity to both the men's chambers, so it wasn't too difficult."

"And what follows after this?"

"I'm not at all sure. Let the public get over the

surprises of hearing these medical geniuses say their pieces, then I'll work out the next move. I think, though, it might be a good idea if tonight I release the final message congratulating the world for having had the good sense to listen to my advice—"

Albert turned as, with a tap on the door, the housemaid entered. She was looking vaguely disturbed.

"There's a police sergeant to see you, sir." She looked at Albert anxiously. "Says it's most urgent."

Albert's expression changed. "A—a police sergeant? Oh? Well, I—er—can't think why. Have him come in, Annie."

"Yessir. Right away, sir."

In a matter of moments the detective-sergeant had been ushered in and the door closed. Albert did his best to appear at his ease, but his heart was thudding painfully.

"Do you know a young lady by the name of Vera Patricia Simpkins, sir?" the sergeant asked gravely.

"I should." Albert felt a surge of relief. This surely could have nothing to do with his Voice performance. "She is my eldest daughter."

"I'm sorry to hear that, sir, because I've rather bad news for you. You will be her mother, madam?"

"Yes, of course I am. Sergeant, what is it? What's wrong?"

The detective-sergeant told the story and left behind him two stunned, silent people. They had no idea how long it was before they looked at each other again.

"It's—it's beyond all reason!" Emily whispered,

her eyes staring blankly. "She just *couldn't* have been killed, not by lightning or anything. There's been no storm. And what was she doing in a recreation ground? She ought to have been coming home...."

Albert was silent, his hands dangling limply between his knees.

"Albert, I'm speaking to you!" Emily's voice was shrill. "How could it have happened?"

"I don't know, Emmy," Albert whispered. "I just don't know. The thing's beyond me...." He got up and held his forehead for a moment. "I'd better do as the sergeant asks and go and—and identify the body. My God, identify the *body*! Of all the ghastly, inhuman tasks to have to perform! How did this damnable thing happen, Emmy? Vee may have been a nuisance and headstrong in some ways, but she was ours after all...."

Emily could not answer, she was too choked with tears. Albert gave her shoulder a gentle pat and then headed for the door. When he reached it he glanced back.

"Don't tell the kids yet," he cautioned. "It'll have to be broken gently...."

Then he was on his way, his meal and intended world-broadcast completely forgotten.

* * * * * * *

For two days Albert and Emily were too stunned by the reaction of Vera's death to think clearly. The children had been told, and in consequence moved about in subdued silence, wondering in their still immature minds what had really overtaken their sister. They were not the only ones who wondered either. The brains of Scotland Yard were baffled, and the surgeon's p.m. report did not clear the air, either.

Chief-Inspector Dawson, who had the case in hand, willingly admitted that he was up against it—not to his superiors, but to his right-hand man, the detective-sergeant who had broken the grim news to Albert and Emily.

"It doesn't make sense, Harry," Dawson insisted, on the third day—when he had all the facts before him. "This girl sat in the recreation ground on a perfectly quiet summer evening. There was nobody about, as far as we can ascertain, no sign of a storm, and, even less of electricity—yet this poor girl was scorched and blinded by electrical energy! The only person who was at all hostile towards her was her former boyfriend, but he's got a water-tight alibi."

"Maybe the Scientific Division could help?" the detective-sergeant suggested. "I know they're pretty preoccupied with the Conqueror's Voice problem at present, but they might find time to give us a hand."

"Yes, maybe it's worth trying," Dawson conceded, and switched on the intercom....

Accordingly the Scientific Division delegated certain of its members to investigate the recreation ground where Vera had met her death, and they went to work with apparatus that was not within the province of an ordinary homicide man. Just the same, they did not discover anything abnormal. Indeed, the only discovery they did make was something in the field of normal police work: a middle-aged man had been seen in the recreation-ground about the time Vera had met her death—and this piece of information came from two employees of a painting firm who had been paint-spraying a building overlooking the recreation-ground about the time of Vera's decease. They gave the information voluntarily, having gathered from the newspapers and broadcasting media that the police were up against it. The reason why they could remember this lone individual so well was because of the queer boxlike object he had been carrying, depending from his shoulder by a leather strap.

With this slender clue to go upon, Chief-Inspector Dawson set his trained investigators to work. Their task was to trace the man with the queer box at all costs. That queer box might explain many things. So inquiry began—relentless, thorough, crosschecked every inch of the way.

Of all this hue and cry Albert Simpkins was in ignorance, of course. He, Emily, and the family attended Vera's funeral and then life picked itself up again because it had to. The inquest on Vera had been postponed pending further police investigation. The Coroner had declared himself far from satisfied....

Albert was the first to realize the wisdom of the statement that one cannot live with the dead, so gradually he resumed his former course and watched with interest the trend of world events. Wholesale jettisoning of armaments was still in progress, and a date had been fixed for the simultaneous sinking or blowing up of all ships of war. It was definitely time, and beyond it, for his final announcement to the world through the medium of the Voice.

So a week after Vera's funeral, the Conqueror's Voice spoke for the last time, swamping all normal radio waves as usual and giving engineers everywhere more gray hairs as they tried to fathom how the trick was done. The message was brief and to the point. Albert heard it in the lounge of his own home in the quiet of that summer evening. Emily, morosely silent, heard it too. The children—the younger ones—were out playing and entirely disinterested, and Ethel was engaged with a badminton match.

"You have shown great wisdom, my friends of Earth," the rich basso-profundo proclaimed. "I promised you a reward for acting with sanity, and that reward cannot long be delayed. In your society you have many problems—medical, social, and political. You will find that these problems will be solved by the geniuses who will rise amongst you.... I shall never speak to you again, but I shall always be watching over your destiny, and for your own sake the warning I gave when I first contacted you still holds good. Live peacefully and strive towards scientific emancipation. If you do not, you stand in danger of destruction. Remember, I shall live longer than any of you. I shall always be watching—always."

The Voice ceased. Albert relaxed a little and smiled to himself. His forehead was moist with the emotion of the moment. He caught Emily's glance.

"Satisfactory?" he asked quietly.

"I suppose so. I'm thankful, somehow, that you won't have to use that Voice again. Every time I hear it, I picture the scientists trying to work out where it comes from. Let's hope this is a case of third time lucky."

"You have no appreciation of what I have done for the world, have you, Emmy?" Albert looked at her seriously. "You haven't yet realized that a simple cinema projectionist has made himself the dictator of the Earth and yet lived a more or less normal life as well. By my own ingenuity I have compelled warmongers and agitators to toe the line. I have brought peace to Earth, and shall yet bring untold benefit. You haven't comprehended one bit of it, have you?"

"It's one of those things which can't *be* realized, Albert—at least, not all at once."

Emily looked up as Annie, the housemaid, appeared in the doorway.

"Chief-Inspector Dawson, sir," she announced, looking at Albert. And this time he did not flinch. Be something about Vera, of course.

"Thanks, Annie. Ask him in here, will you?"

Dawson entered a moment later, shook hands cordially enough, then settled on the settee as Albert motioned to it. There followed a brief pause, then:

"The purpose of my call is private, Mr. Simpkins. I must inform you of that."

"I hadn't realized," Emily apologized, struggling to her feet. "I'll just leave you to—"

"Stay where you are, Emmy," Albert interrupted, and to the inspector he added: "Whatever concerns our late daughter is a joint affair, inspector."

"I realize that, sir, but this is a rather unexpected angle on your daughter's death, and is intended for your ears alone."

"I prefer that you speak openly."

Dawson shrugged. "Up to you, sir. I've a question or two to ask. Would you mind telling me what you were doing in Saint John's Recreation Ground on the day of your daughter's death?"

Albert stared blankly. Emily gave a start and looked at him with a peculiarly incredulous gaze.

"Saint John's," the inspector explained, "is the name of the recreation-ground where your daughter died. You will be aware of that."

"Certainly I am. It has been mentioned enough times."

Albert rubbed his lower lip uncertainly. He had been in the recreation ground in order to put the two medical men under the influence of his apparatus, but he had not noticed the *name* of the recreation ground. From the sound of things it must have been—Saint John's.

"You are sure there is no mistake?" he asked, and the inspector smiled dourly.

"None at all, sir. I wouldn't be here otherwise. I'm sure there's a perfectly reasonable explanation."

"And I'm equally sure your facts are wrong!" Albert retorted. "Why on earth should I be in Saint John's Recreation Ground unknown to my daughter? It doesn't begin to make sense."

"Oh, I don't know," Dawson said disarmingly. "It is not uncommon for two relatives to be in one park at the same time and yet not meet each other. It happens every day. The awkward part in this instance is that you were not just passing *through* the recreation ground. You remained there quite a while, in a position well concealed from any chance passerby."

"Then how, does anybody know I was there?"

"So you were there, Mr. Simpkins?"

"I didn't say so!" Albert snapped. "Stop putting answers into my mouth, can't you!"

"You were observed by painters working on a house overlooking the ground. You were there quite half an hour before your daughter met her death."

"Albert, what does this mean?" came Emily's tremulous voice. "*Were* you in that recreation ground?"

"Without a shadow of a doubt," Dawson declared flatly. "Come now, Mr. Simpkins, as the girl's father you can surely give me some co-operation? I'm not trying to pin anything on you: I am merely asking what you were doing in the park."

"I—I went in there for a rest," Albert said desperately. "I'd been tramping about all day and I was tired. It was very hot, if you remember, and—"

"Why had you been tramping all day?"

"Why? In the course of my business—"

"From all accounts, Mr. Simpkins, and we check these things very carefully, you are of more or less independent means. If not that, then you exist on the royalties of scientific inventions, and so forth. Not that there is any harm in that."

"Thanks for the concession!"

"Which means," Dawson explained patiently, "that a man in your position has no need to tramp about all day, especially with a heavy-looking box hanging from his shoulder."

"Box?" Albert repeated dully.

"That is what it looked like to the painters opposite. They said you looked rather like an old-fashioned hurdy-gurdy man."

"They must be confusing me with somebody else. I had no box."

"Yes you had, Mr. Simpkins, and you are not being confused with anybody else. My men have checked back on everything. They know all your moves, your calls in the telephone kiosk, your brief lunch at the Sunset Café—everything. One can never really move unobserved, you know. There are watching taxi-drivers, newspaper-vendors, street cleaners—all manner of people who remember, and speak."

Silence. Albert looked desperately towards the gathered evening, towards his locked laboratory workshop. The inspector sat back and waited.

"Very well," Albert said at last, "I'll tell you. I am a scientific inventor. The box referred to is for making tests of the atmosphere, and so forth. I'm trying to find a way of controlling our erratic climate. Given time, I'll do it."

"Very interesting," Dawson commented. "In that

case I'd be glad if I could see the box. I'd like our Scientific Division to examine it.

"Certainly not! Why should I show a secret process which it has taken me years to perfect?"

"Mr. Simpkins, you know perfectly well that Scotland Yard is above suspicion. You should also appreciate by now that your position is not a favorable one. Understand this, sir: you were the only person in the recreation ground anywhere near your daughter at the time she met her death!"

"Albert, you didn't—" Emily had risen to her feet in dreadful doubt. "It wasn't because of what Vee said she'd do? It wasn't because you quarreled that—"

"For God's sake, Emmy, shut up!" Albert snapped.

Dawson looked from one to the other with his flinty eyes.

"Because of what she said she'd do?" he repeated softly. "Quarrel? Might I ask what you mean by that, madam?"

"Your questions are being addressed to me—not my wife," Albert said curtly.

"My questions are addressed where they can do the most good, sir. What were you about to say, Mrs. Simpkins?"

"Er—nothing much. That is— Well, Vera squabbled with her dad the night before she.... She was a head-strong sort of girl at the best of times."

"Squabbles have a basic reason, Mrs. Simpkins. What was the cause of the trouble?"

"None of your business!" Albert answered.

"It so happens that it is, sir. It would appear that there might have been a motive for your being in the recreation ground. That, so far, has been the one thing lacking. Why *did* you quarrel with your daughter?"

"She was impudent, and I had to reprimand her. As was her custom, she sulked afterwards."

"And what was it she said she would do?"

"I've said all I'm going to say, inspector. This is my home, not a law court."

Dawson reflected and then got to his feet. "You do not seem to realize that I am trying to help you out of a ticklish position, sir. I cannot force you to answer questions if you don't wish to, of course, but you'd be wiser if you did. Now regarding that box— Will you permit me to have it, or not?"

"No! And that's final."

"I came prepared for that." Dawson withdrew a search warrant from his pocket and held it out. "This legally entitles me to search where I wish and appropriate whatever I deem fit to help the case on hand. I felt beforehand that that box would cause you to hesitate, so here is my authority. Will you let me have it voluntarily, or must my men do it? I have only to call them from the patrol car outside."

Albert's troubled eyes strayed unconsciously to the French windows and beyond them to the workshop-laboratory. Dawson glanced towards the building and smiled tautly.

"Thank you for the lead," he said dryly. "Are you going to help, or not?"

"I'll get it," Albert growled, and went outside. It seemed to him, and his thoughts were completely out of hand, that it would be the lesser of two evils to get the "box of tricks" than allow Dawson to see the complication of the laboratory. The preservation of the secret of the Conqueror was still the dominant necessity in Albert's mind.

To his satisfaction Dawson did not follow him up: he remained by the French windows, watching. When at last Albert brought the box into the lounge and set it on the table, the inspector looked at it curiously. It was plain, when Albert opened the lid and revealed the queer clocklike mechanism and instruments within that the man of the law was not a scientist.

"For atmosphere testing, you say?"

"Yes, I don't intend to explain how it works. If your Scientific Division at the Yard is so clever, let them find out for themselves."

"They will, sir, be assured of that." Dawson heaved the box on to his shoulder after Albert had closed the lid. "Thank you for answering my questions, sir, and I am sorry to have been so persistent. I'll get in touch with you again later."

CHAPTER NINE

The lounge seemed dreadfully quiet to Albert when he came back into it, nor could he avoid Emily's intently watching eyes.

"Dammit, woman, you don't think I'd murder my own daughter, do you?" he demanded abruptly.

"Oh, Albert, I don't know what *to* think, and that's the truth! It keeps on going through my mind that this Voice business means more to you than anything else in the world. You love the power it gives you, and you preen yourself with the thought of how you have brought peace to the world. I believe you'd sacrifice anything to keep your secret. Vee was the one person likely to upset everything."

"So you believe I silenced her?"

Emily did not answer, but she looked away and through the French windows. She started when Albert's hands clamped down on her shoulders.

"Tell me how I did it, then!" he challenged. "By what means could I blast the life out of her with electricity?"

"Albert, for God's sake—!" Emily gave him a tearful glance. "Do you have to put it so brutally?"

"Yes I do! This is a brutal business, and I'm on the

wrong end of it! I'm asking you again: how *could* I have killed Vee in the manner described?"

"I don't know. I'm not scientific like you. But I think you could do anything with electricity. Anything! Look how you made that Voice speak, using enough power to swamp the ordinary radio stations. Something atomic maybe. Oh, I just don't know."

Albert released Emily suddenly and turned away. He plunged his hands in his trouser pockets and mooched to the French windows.

"This is a damnable thing to happen," he muttered, half to himself. "Just at the very climax when I have everything right. If things come unstuck now, if the world gets to know it has been hoaxed into becoming peaceful...."

"Never *mind* the world!" Emily shouted hysterically. "What about Vee? In heavens' name, Albert, why did you have to go that far?"

Albert looked at her steadily. "I didn't. I keep telling you. The whole thing's a damnable coincidence. I'm sorry you haven't more trust in me."

Emily was silent. She had, to a certain extent, spoken in the haste of the moment, utterly uncertain what to do between renewed grief and the shock of finding her husband mysteriously involved in Vera's death. But Albert did not take any of these things into account. He saw only distrust—even hatred.

"I think," he said quietly, "it might be better if I left home for awhile and went to live in a hotel. We're liable to get on each other's nerves. Later, when things have quieted down, we can get together again. My good intentions towards humanity will have to wait for awhile. I can't do anything without my box of tricks, anyway."

"How much are the Scotland Yard scientists likely to discover concerning that apparatus?" Emily asked, low-voiced.

"I don't know. They're not fools, obviously, but I doubt if they will grasp the scientific principle of that thing, since it is my secret...."

But in this Albert greatly underestimated the acumen of the boffins of Scotland Yard's Scientific Division. His box of tricks, handed in by Dawson for examination, proved to be one of the most intriguing exhibits they had ever had to examine. They spent nearly a week studying the instrument, and at the end of this time their report was handed in to Chief-Inspector Dawson. He read it, puzzled over it—for he was not a scientific man—checked back on certain points with the head of the Division, and then at length he asked if Douglas Marshall—successor to the ill-starred Forsythe—would step in and have a word with him the moment he was available.... Which was exactly what Marshall did.

"I feel, Doug," Dawson said, as the scientific investigator seated himself, "that we may be on to something here, by the sheerest accident. First, though, how far have you got with the investigation of the Conqueror's Voice?"

"I haven't got anywhere definite, but I'm still living in hopes."

"That's what I thought. Well, then, here's something interesting. I'm looking into the business of Vera Simpkins, who was recently—"

"Blasted to death by electricity in an empty recreation ground. I know the details since my men investigated."

"Exactly so; but I don't think you are aware that the girl's father was in the recreation ground at the time of her death, and that in his possession he had a curious scientific instrument with an atomic battery. Your Division has been studying the instrument, and the upshot is that it can project a stream of deadly electrical energy over a considerable distance, and can also induce mesmerism."

"Oh?" Marshall wrinkled his forehead. "Sounds a kind of futuristic gadget."

"Your Division says it is the conception of a scientific and engineering genius! Now," Dawson continued, handing over the report for Marshall to study, "one of the outstanding problems in your particular case is—or has been—the weird behavior of certain public figures. It isn't an impossible hypothesis that their antics might have been caused by hypnotism, electrically amplified by just such an instrument as this."

"Could be," Marshall mused, finishing his brief study of the report.

"On the other hand, by simple conversion, this instrument could—as you see on the report—project electrical energy of such high voltage as to bring death. It could have killed Vera Simpkins...."

"You mean," Marshall said slowly, "that the girl's father may be behind the hypnosis of certain public figures?"

"I mean more than that. He may be the Conqueror's Voice!"

Marshall looked undecided. "Is it possible that things could fall right into our lap like this?"

"I think so. You are looking for somebody who is an amateur—that fact has been stressed for long enough. In the past week, whilst your Division has been examining this apparatus, I have been checking up on Albert Simpkins very thoroughly. For many years he was a chief projectionist in a small-time cinema, and after that he became a cleaner in a laboratory for guided missiles. Laboratory 9, as a matter of fact. I have also found that he did, at one period, prior to the coming of the Conqueror's Voice, purchase considerable quantities of electrical equipment. I don't see how we can ignore so many plain facts.... I gather he has some kind of private laboratory adjoining his home. A search of it—official, of course—might prove very interesting. For my own part, I'm going to pin him on a murder charge, because I'm convinced he used that queer apparatus of his to bring about the death of his daughter."

"That is your pigeon," Marshall said, "but for *my* own part I'm interested in what you have told me about him. I'll make all the necessary moves to have his laboratory investigated."

* * * * * * *

And Marshall did not waste any time about it either. That same afternoon he and Inspector Dawson called at the Simpkins home to find Emily present but not Albert.

"Where is he?" Dawson asked ominously. "I hope he's had the good sense not to leave town at this juncture?"

"No, no, he hasn't done anything like that. He's not the sort to run away, inspector. You'll find him at the Climax Hotel in Brunning Place. We—er—sort of didn't get along too well together after the other night, when you had called."

"I have here a search warrant," Marshall put in. "It entitles me to examine the laboratory-workshop which is outside there."

Emily gave a wild look around her. "But—but I don't think you can get in. My husband has the key, and—"

"Get him on the, phone, madam," Marshall interrupted. "I'll very soon speak to him."

With nervous movements Emily did as she was told, and Marshall did the rest. What Albert said at the other end of the wire was not audible, but Marshall certainly left no doubt as to what he intended doing.

"Up to you, Mr. Simpkins. Either come over right away and unlock this laboratory of yours, or I'll be compelled to break it in. Those are my orders."

The upshot was that Albert arrived within fifteen minutes—flustered and angry. He opened up the laboratory and then stood waiting, until Marshall glanced at him briefly over his shoulder.

"I'll be here some time, sir. I'd suggest you return to the house. The inspector wishes to speak to you."

Grim-faced, Albert came back into the lounge, to find the level eyes of Dawson upon him. Emily was nearby, tearful and anxious.

"Your wife has just been telling me, sir, that you and your daughter quarreled because she knew an important secret of yours—"

Albert started and then glared at Emily. "So that's the best you can do, Emmy? Give me away!"

"I—I didn't mean to, Albert. He tricked me into it."

"And I'm not apologizing!" Dawson snapped. "Your daughter knew that you were the Conqueror's Voice, and it was essential you stop her knowledge going any further."

Albert remained completely silent, his fists clenched at his sides and his eyes roving the inspector's square face.

"Not," Dawson added, "that that side of the business is of interest to me. That is Inspector Marshall's province, which is why he is now examining your laboratory. My duty, Albert Simpkins, is to charge you with the murder of your daughter, Vera Patricia Simpkins, and to warn you that anything you say will be taken down and may be used in evidence."

"This gets beyond belief," Albert whispered, shaking his head wearily. "That I should kill Vee— It's utterly inhuman, inspector! Haven't you any natural, paternal feelings at all?"

"How I feel doesn't enter into it. I'm interpreting the

law, and our evidence is complete."

"*What* evidence?" Albert demanded. "I had no possible way of murdering Vera. And I didn't murder her, anyway."

"You had an instrument capable of two possibilities—one producing hypnotism, and the other the generation of an electrical voltage capable of bringing instant death, sufficient to produce on your daughter the severe burns which killed her."

"Look, I tell you—"

"It is not my purpose to argue, Mr. Simpkins. My part ends with arresting you, so I must ask you to come along." Albert hesitated, looking at his wife—but she turned away slowly to hide her emotion. Then Marshall came in at the french windows, his face grim.

"Well? Finished poking and prying?" Albert demanded of him.

"I have certainly obtained all the information I need," the Yard man answered. "But there is much confirmatory evidence which the law will require before bringing against you the strangest charge in history."

Albert laughed shortly. "Have to be quick, won't you? I'm already indicted for murder."

* * * * * * *

With the law nailing him down, Albert Simpkins could move no further. The benefits he had intended conferring on mankind could not mature. Not that mankind knew anything of this, for it was a case of "what you've never had you never miss."

The law, however, had only taken the first step. Here was a legal matter of profound complexity since it involved two counts—the one murder presumed, and the other the Conqueror's Voice. Legal wiseacres averred that the charge of murder be withheld from trial until the facts concerning the Conqueror's Voice had been established, for here was a matter of world-wide concern which might well miss explanation if Simpkins were sentenced before having a chance to elucidate the scientific details of his extraordinary feat.

To the Assistant Commissioner for the Scientific Division, Marshall gave all the details of his own side of the case. "In that laboratory of Simpkins', sir, I discovered all the necessary equipment for remote control. That in, itself would not mean anything, only I noticed that the control register on the output had been set for one hundred thousand miles, which in turn was linked to radar devices for pinpointing some object or other. We know already that a guided missile is—or was—producing the Conqueror's Voice, and we know its distance. The coincidence cannot be admitted. It means that Simpkins has been controlling something at a hundred thousand miles distance."

"The court will not accept that as it stands," the A.C. said, thinking. "We have to produce the final pieces of evidence—the cause of the Voice, the identity of the person responsible for the Voice. A full scientific dossier, in fact. If only Forsythe had survived...."

"Yes, sir, but he didn't," Marshall interrupted. "Therefore I suggest I go into space in the same way he did and bring back all the essential details which the court will require. As you are aware, Simpkins himself just won't tell us a thing."

"And you are prepared to take that risk, knowing what happened to Forsythe?"

"We don't really know *what* happened to him," Forsythe replied, shrugging. "In any event, I'm willing to take the chance to try and finish things off. I don't doubt that the dean of Laboratory Nine can fix things up for me just as he did for Forsythe."

To which the Assistant Commissioner raised no more objections. From here on the whole thing was Marshall's responsibility, and his first move was to contact the dean of Laboratory 9 and secure his co-operation. It was freely given, not because the dean was willing to have Albert Simpkins' great deception exposed, but because he would get nowhere by obstructing the wishes of the all-powerful law. A missile would be prepared, Marshall would have to go into training as had his predecessor—and that would be that.

Meantime, Chief-Inspector Dawson was also gathering what other facts he could to lend weight to the prosecution when the time came. His particular objection—about which he could do exactly nothing—was to the amendment in the law which made it possible, due to the extraordinary circumstances, for Albert Simpkins' trial for murder to be held in abeyance until he had answered the wider charge of world-deception. The whole thing was a complete anomaly of law.

The public had no idea what was happening. A small announcement had stated that Albert had been arrested for the murder of his daughter, but nothing more had been said after that. The Yard completely clamped down on all news connecting Albert with the Voice until the facts were beyond all dispute. And Emily, Ethel, and the two younger children? The disgrace which had descended upon them, and the fact that Albert was no longer able to bring in money by means of his peculiar scientific gadgets, had led Emily to sell up the big house and move to one such as they had had before Albert's excursion into "big things."

She settled the three children in new schools, changed the surname, then sat tight and hoped for the best. Now and again she was permitted to see Albert, and found him bitter and tight-lipped. At other times she was preoccupied with his solicitor, who was building up what defense he could against both the murder charge and the more complicated one of "false pretences."

Some weeks passed—weeks of training for Douglas Marshall, until, as it had come for Forsythe, so it came from him to make the dive into the void. He accepted the zero hour with the same matter-of-fact calmness as his predecessor and, one quiet evening in the waning summer, his projectile swept skywards and flattened him to his padded seat by the drag of the escape velocity.

In general his actions were a repeat of those of Forsythe. He radioed his experiences back to Earth on a secret waveband, the messages being picked up by both Laboratory Nine and the technicians in the Scotland Yard Scientific Division. It appeared that Marshall was not having much trouble in making the trip. Everything was going according to plan, and his radar equipment had already re-echoed from the missile flying at 100,000 miles from Earth. Indeed, he had had *two* echoes, which could only mean he had also contacted Forsythe's own projectile, held in the gravitational field of the mystery missile itself.

So Marshall hurtled onwards—eating, sleeping, cursing his cramped quarters or marveling at the unending majesty of space. Until at last he came within telescopic range of his goal. For a brief while he beheld the two missiles close together sweeping on their endless 7,000-mile-an-hour orbit, and, as Forsythe had done, he began the same "catching up" maneuver that finally brought him alongside both missiles. Eventually he managed to weave his way into the fair space between them, and here his vessel anchored, chained by the projectiles to either side of him.

It was now a matter for a spacesuit and that sickening dive into sheer space. Marshall did not shrink from it. He took the plunge as Forsythe had done, and found himself weightless in sheer infinity, the vast, terrifying bowl of Earth hanging somewhere on his left. His training had shown him how to pilot himself in non-gravity fields, how to impel himself by the recoil of the small-sized rockets fastened to his back. He activated the firing mechanism and immediately shot forward, grabbing at the supports round Forsythe's missile as he collided with it.

Once inside the machine he found it empty, the airlock wide open. It was no more than he had expected. Whatever had struck Forsythe down had evidently been aboard the other missile, the mystery one presumably made by Albert Simpkins. So Marshall took the second plunge, fought his way to the top deck, and then paused for a moment to recover his breath. It was strange to be without any sense of motion and yet be moving at 7,000 miles an hour. Yet such was the case. The only clue to his speed lay in Earth itself gradually shifting position.

So, with this simple lesson in Relativity driven well home, Marshall finally clambered down the ladder into Simpkins' projectile, and at the base of the ladder he fell over something frozen into complete solidity by the vacuum of space. His torch beam revealed a deflated spacesuit caked in frost. Chipping some of the ice from the face-visor, he looked through the frost-split glass upon a perfectly preserved face. It was Forsythe, staring fixedly in death, showing no sign of mortification due to the everlasting vacuum.

Marshall turned away at last, decided in his own mind that he would leave Forsythe's body in its airless tomb. It was as sane a burial as any and one where "moth and rust" could not corrupt. Then he turned his attention to those plainly homemade instruments which had attracted Forsythe before atomic bomb explosions had made an end of him.

Marshall's search was a long and detailed one,

conducted with the thoroughness of an experienced scientific engineer. He found that all the equipment was within sealed cowlings, evidently against the possibility of space getting at them—which indeed had happened thanks to Forsythe's advent.

The moment Marshall removed the cowlings, he saw frost leap to the naked wires and complicated electrical circuits, frost which quickly vanished as his electrically-heated gloves began to investigate further.

By degrees he went through a process of dismantling, smiling tautly to himself as first one piece of equipment and then another made sense to his analytical mind. Until finally, after a couple of hours of hard work, he had all the stuff he needed completely free, and thereupon commenced to transport it to his own machine. This was by no means a difficult task. All he had to do was heave the various pieces of equipment through the airlock, each piece being almost weightless, and then push them in a kind of chain ahead of him across the narrow gulf of space to his own vessel. It made him think for a moment that, in space, engineering could be a very simple job. One man alone would be able to support a fifty-story building without any strain whatsoever.

By degrees he got each piece of equipment into his own control room; then he closed the lock, brought up the heat and air pressure to normal, and rid himself of his spacesuit. All he had to wait for now was for the equipment to thaw out, and then he could make a detailed analysis as he returned home.

This was certainly his intention, but it did not work out that way. He had only just set the course for home and satisfied himself that the equipment was ready for scrutiny when he became aware of intense light throughout the control room. Surprised, he looked about him, thinking for the moment that somehow direct sunlight was hitting him. No, that could not be the explanation. This light was somehow inside the control-room itself, apparently supported in the air by some mysterious means or other. A curious globe it appeared to be, drifting in front of the control board and becoming brighter with every moment. Fascinated, Marshall stared at it—just as ill-fated Vera Simpkins had stared in the quiet of the recreation ground until her sight had been destroyed.

Marshall acted with more sanity than Vera. Suddenly realizing that the intensifying glare was hurting his eyes, he reached up and snatched a pair of purple goggles, normally used when the sunlight was too intense. This enabled him to look upon the blinding manifestation more closely, and he could now detect a curious darker center in the midst of the effulgence.... This darker center was pulsating back and forth, just as if it were a beating heart.

The glare increased, even through the goggles. Petrified in his supine position, Marshall kept on gazing at the manifestation, the various pieces of equipment around him. It had dawned upon him by now that this horrible thing of light was sentient and deadly. He could feel electrified radiations pulsating from it, sweeping over his exposed skin with the keen-ness of a razor's edge.

"In heaven's name, what are you?" he gasped at lost. "How did you get in here?"

No answer. Only the intensifying brilliance and the building up of electrical voltage. Marshall writhed, but he could not move from his cramped position. He knew electricity was slowly blasting the life out of him, and as he did so he remembered Vera Simpkins and her strange death. He knew now with everything that was in him that what had happened to her was precisely what was happening to him. In that case, it could *not* have been her father who had killed her! He was in jail, 100,000 miles away. He could not be responsible for *this*.

Marshall knew he was dying as his little world became soaked in unfathomable, tingling brilliance, so bright that his eyes stung even behind the purple lenses. Even so, with what strength remained to him, he turned to the radio and switched it on.

"Marshall calling Earth!" he cried frantically, when the pilot light showed the equipment was working. "I am being attacked by some kind of electrical entity— Will never reach home. Have—have all details concerning Conqueror's Voice. Messages are recorded on tape and remote-controlled—Albert Simpkins is not guilty of murder. Electrical entity which is—is attacking me could also have attacked Vera Simpkins. I don't know what it is. I—I—"

Marshall could get no further. He was tearing apart

as the electrical voltage rose to unbearable intensity. The world of inconceivable brightness dimmed before him and relapsed into blackness. But still the blaze of light continued until the very instruments began to shatter apart under the electric vibration. After they had gone, the projectile also literally shivered itself into dust.

But this was not all. The hovering entity, brighter than the brightest star, moved position slightly and appeared to pass through the midst of the two other missiles nearby—Forsythe's and Albert Simpkins'. When the entity moved again these two vessels had also disappeared. The brightness began to fade and, gradually, the void was as dark as it had ever been— but of missiles or corpses, there was not a trace.

* * * * * * *

On the night side of Earth astronomers saw the brilliant spot 100,000 miles from Earth and vainly tried to imagine what it could be. Certainly not a star at such close quarters, for it had no gravity. Then before they could conjecture further it disappeared. Perhaps an atomic bomb from the disarmament had latently exploded. Perhaps.... Nobody knew for certain, and Scotland Yard and the scientists could only guess and have dire misgivings.

The odd thing was that Marshall's gasping last message to Earth was never received! The tremendous electrical field set up by the unknown something in space had completely erased his transmission, so nobody was any the wiser. Indeed, everybody concerned with the Marshall venture was profoundly disturbed as no word came from him and the reports of that evanescent "star" came from various quarters.

The morning after the "star's" advent, the A.C. of the Scientific Division called a conference of scientists and police connected with the Voice investigation.

"I think, gentleman," he said, his voice tired with disappointment, "that we have again to write up failure and tragedy. Our good friend Marshall has not communicated for nearly fourteen hours and that can only mean that the worst has happened. The astronomers report a light of intense brilliance at approximately the point where Marshall was, so just anything can have happened, as it did to Forsythe."

The dean of Laboratory Nine, who had been asked to attend the conference, gave a grim shake of his head.

"It couldn't be atomic bombs this time, as it was in the case of Forsythe. It was something else. After all, we know little of what lies in space—perhaps sinister forces quite invisible to us. I believe, as I have always believed, that we should take these abortive efforts at condemning Simpkins as a sign that they are not to be. He has done much for the world; for heaven's sake let it rest at that."

"To which the answer is still the same," the A.C. sighed. "I have a public duty to perform, and we have enough evidence to show that Simpkins had something to do with the Voice. Marshall would have completed that evidence. As it is, what facts we have must be placed before the court."

"The whole thing is wrong," the dean muttered. "Here in our midst we have this great benefactor, the simple man with the spark of genius and humanity— and yet we nail him down for bringing peace to the world and supposedly murdering his own daughter! It is a sorry reflection on the elasticity of justice!"

To which the Assistant Commissioner had nothing further to say. Another venture into space was out of the question. Two useful lives had been lost, and it would be absolute insanity to try yet again.

"We must work with what we have," the A.C. said at last, rising. "Thank you, gentlemen, for attending, and for the work you have put into this extremely intricate matter. The rest is up to the court."

So Albert Simpkins was brought to trial—and by now it had become general knowledge that he was also implicated as the possible creator of the Conqueror's Voice. This latter fact had stirred public interest throughout the world since few, except the more scientific, had the remotest conception of how he could have projected his all-powerful messages from such a tremendous distance.

And Albert still remained silent, a disappointed and completely disillusioned man. The only friend he seemed to have left was Jerome Lennox, his defense lawyer, also a fair scientist with a good grip of essentials.

In accordance with the specially amended law to suit the abnormal circumstances, the first indictment was not for murder, but for "false pretences and misrepresentation." This was a ridiculous misnomer to describe a scientific trick that had hoaxed the world, yet in legal phraseology it was regarded as quite befitting.

Martin Shaw, the prosecuting counsel, was plainly quite disinclined to show his victim any mercy when he opened the case against Albert. Tall, arrogant, vinegar-faced, he threw out his allegations piecemeal, pinning Albert occasionally with a dramatically outthrust finger.

"Ladies and gentlemen of the jury, you have been made aware of the amazing facts of this case, the sinister story of a quiet man suddenly overwhelmed with a desire for power. I have explained to you how, to satisfy this lust for grandeur, he conceived the astounding idea of making the world obey his commands! Not having enough at that time to put his grandiose scheme into operation, he invented a deadly instrument, which, our experts assure us, can produce hypnotism over a wide range by a strange process of 'sympathizing' with the victim's brain frequencies.... His first victim was his helpless daughter, whom he compelled to perform some undignified, ridiculous act to satisfy his own whim.

"Following this, he forced his brother to give him money; and not satisfied with this, he tackled industrial leaders and forced them, too, to pay him for inventions he had sold to them many years before. With this money he built a missile, having learned all about it by becoming a cleaner in Laboratory Nine, where secret long-range missiles are constructed. He acted like an intellectual parasite, and used secrets intended only for scientific experts.

"So, finally, he hurled forth into space a missile. He controlled it by radio—a not unusual accomplishment in these days—and within that missile was a recording mechanism upon which had already *been* recorded three messages, which later reached mankind. The prisoner had become a god, a ruler of men, and he had nothing to do but sit back and laugh whilst the world danced to his tune."

Martin Shaw paused, breathed hard down his nose, and then looked at Albert as he sat morosely listening.

"We have pieced together the strange character of this man, a man determined to have the world at his feet, a man who has cost countless thousands their livelihood by enforcing world disarmament...."

Albert was still silent—but he could foresee the end.

CHAPTER TEN

The Prosecuting Counsel gave Albert a long, bitter look and then continued:

"I am no more in sympathy with armed might than anybody else, but I do take the broad view that even armaments mean a good living for millions in the community. This man, Albert Simpkins, has destroyed all that with his damnable ego...."

"And what else did he do? He forced public figures to make idiots of themselves! And why? So he could laugh in derision at those whom he imagined had looked down upon him in less exalted days. This is not a *normal* man who is on trial, ladies and gentlemen. He is an egomaniac with a scientific streak, and because of that he is dangerous beyond measure...."

At the close of which, and considering his long preceding speech, the Prosecuting Counsel was considerably short of breath. The jury regarded him woodenly and the judge shifted his notes. Albert himself remained unmoved, the same dull light still in his eyes. But they began to brighten a little as the Defense Counsel moved in to make his summing up.

"With all respect to my learned colleague," Jerome

Lennox said, "he has, with commendable accuracy, singled out all the unpleasant factors and dropped the happier ones overboard— So, ladies and gentlemen, I would refresh your memory on certain points. The prosecution refers vaguely to a missile hurled into space, said missile containing all manner of strange instruments and, in particular, a recording apparatus with a high power atomic transmitter. But where *is* this missile? Can we not see it? Have some *evidence* of it? A photograph, maybe, or a telescopic print? No! We are just asked to accept that it is so and that, I submit, is ridiculous!

"Secondly, no mention is made of the good that has been brought to us through disarmament and the removal of war-hysteria from the world. Nobody says anything about the *useful* side of the prisoner's hypnotic efforts. That he has caused hypnosis we accept as a fact because he has admitted it, and his special instrument for the job is well capable of producing the effects outlined. But where has been the harm? It has been shown that in regard to money matters, the prisoner merely demanded that which was his due—and got it. What of the hypnotized financiers who gave so freely to charity? What of the two doctors, who recently declared, independently, that they have the absolute cure for consumption and arthritis? Are those hypnotic feats the work of an egomaniac? I say they are not. As for those public figures who were made objects of ridicule, I submit that that was not the basic intention. The *main* purpose was to draw notice to the amazing things people will do when controlled by a will other than their own—and in that direction the plan succeeded.... So, ladies and gentlemen of the jury, you cannot find the prisoner guilty of the charge the prosecution leaves so adroitly in mid-air."

Jerome Lennox went on talking for a considerable time after this, focusing on the evidence which had been given by the various witnesses as the case had proceeded—until at last there was little more the Defense Counsel could say, and he sat down with a grim look of triumph.

The judge coughed, peered round the crowded court, and then adjusted his glasses.

"By virtue of the legislation which has recently been enacted," he said, "we now have to deal with the second charge against the prisoner—namely, that of the murder of his daughter, Vera Patricia Simpkins. I would ask you, Mr. Shaw, to open the case for the prosecution."

There was no diffidence about Shaw as he rose to commence his second attack of the day; and throughout the hot, stuffy hours he went on talking, producing his evidence, hammering home his points with the power begotten of long experience.... Albert Simpkins himself scarcely moved. He appeared to be silently marveling at Martin Shaw's stupendous energy and the evidence he had lined up from unexpected sources.

The painters were called to give their testimony as to what they had seen in the recreation ground. The Yard experts gave their scientific opinion upon the "box of tricks" which had come into their possession. Emily Simpkins was compelled to swear on oath that father and daughter had quarreled over the possibility of Vera going to the police and telling all she knew. The whole grim business was dragged out into the fierce light of publicity, and even the able Jerome Lennox found himself up against it when it came his turn to try and undermine his learned colleague.

"It has not been shown," he insisted, "how this supposed murder was accomplished, m'lud, and upon that I take my stand. The police found no evidence of footprints near the dead girl, and no sign of disturbance. By the Prosecution's own admittance, Simpkins was quite a mile distant from her, hidden by rows of poplar trees. How was he supposed, with his strange instrument, to have produced an electrical phenomenon that killed his daughter? On that the Prosecution is entirely vague. I maintain that the evidence is not strong enough, nor the motive. I beg leave, m'lud, to vary normal procedure far enough to make Albert Simpkins himself my next witness."

"Proceed," the judge assented wearily.

Lennox waited until Simpkins had changed position to the witness stand, then:

"Mr. Simpkins, as the inventor of this strange, electrical hypnotic device, you are best fitted to explain its nature. Do you confirm what the Scotland Yard scientific experts have stated in their evidence?"

"Broadly, yes," Albert agreed quietly. "The instrument can, and does produce electrical hypnosis over a wide area."

"And can it produce an electrical wave of fatal power?"

"If need be, yes, but no use for such power ever occurred to me. One can electrocute oneself with an ordinary electric heater, but one doesn't. It's as simple as that. Unused possibility."

"Would such a wave be capable of reaching your daughter as she sat on the form at the other side of the recreation ground to you?"

"Very easily."

"And what would happen to the trees between you and her?" Lennox asked quickly.

"They would be incinerated, obviously. If my daughter had been burned to death by such an electrical wave, everything else in the track of the wave would also have been burned."

"Thank you," Lennox said quietly; then with a glance at the jury: "That is the main point I wish to make. Further, is not a fact that your presence in the recreation ground, Mr. Simpkins, at the same time as your daughter was pure coincidence?"

"Definitely." Albert nodded. "I had no idea of her movements or intentions. I was in that recreation ground to mentally compel two certain famous doctors to discover the respective cures for arthritis and consumption. You will discover—unless you have already done so—that the chambers of the two gentlemen concerned are within a mile of that recreation ground. I repeat unequivocally that I did not know my daughter was there—and I did not kill her."

Lennox nodded. "Thank you. You may stand down—"

Then, as Albert began to move with the warders behind him, Lennox turned as an usher touched him on the shoulder and handed him a note. He read it through swiftly and looked up with gleaming eyes towards the weary judge.

"M'lud, I beg to bring to your notice certain vital information which has just come to hand, relevant to this case. It is the outcome of a long chance I took on my own behalf and bears upon the matter of the Conqueror's Voice."

"Well?" the judge asked, and waited.

"The Prosecution cannot continue with its charge," Lennox stated deliberately, "because it is based on the fact that Simpkins produced disquiet and disorder through the medium of spoken messages from space—"

"Which is true!" Martin Shaw snapped, jumping up.

"On the face of it, yes. But I have here"—Lennox waved the note he had received—"incontestable evidence that the Conqueror's Voice never came from a human throat! *No human being ever spoke those words!* Therefore no charge, as the Voice is concerned, can be leveled."

"This is ridiculous!" Martin Shaw protested. "M'lud, I resent this line of attack! It is not based upon—"

"You will be good enough to clarify the position, Mr. Lennox," the judge ordered.

"With pleasure, m'lud. When I was briefed for this

case, I naturally made every possible move which might help establish my client's innocence, and one particular move was to commission Alfred Gascoyne, renowned as one of our foremost experts in sound engineering and electromagnetism, to examine the recordings made at Scotland Yard of the Conqueror's Voice. The Yard willingly co-operated and allowed the records to be studied. Gascoyne's considered opinion is that the Voice was not human."

The judge smiled thinly. "A tall order, Mr. Lennox. I heard that Voice myself, and to say that no human ever spoke it is, to say the least of it, fantastic."

"Fantastic, m'lud, but scientific just the same. The fact destroys the Prosecution's case because, as we all know, it is based on the *Voice* specifically, wedded to the assumption that my client either spoke the words himself to a recorder, changing his voice for the purpose, or else hired somebody to do it for him. The Prosecution has not cleared up this point, has not proved that my client spoke, or that any person under his orders did so, either. I now provide the *right* answer—that no human spoke at all."

"Then, who did?" Martin Shaw barked.

Lennox glanced towards the judge. "Mr. Gascoyne himself is outside this courtroom, sir, willing to give evidence as to his findings. Have I your permission to put him on the witness stand?"

"Definitely," the judge assented. "I shall be interested to observe by what wizardry a voice spoke without anybody having been responsible."

There was a stir and murmur in the hot courtroom at the brief respite provided by Gascoyne's arrival. Then he settled at the witness stand and waited—a thin, high-domed individual with darting, light blue eyes. He was sworn in, then Lennox advanced.

"Mr. Gascoyne, I am going to depart from procedure in that I shall not ask you any questions. I will instead instruct you to tell the court in plain language what you discovered in the Voice recordings which I handed over to you."

"I found them incapable of having been spoken by a human being." Gascoyne made his declaration without hesitation. "I converted the sound into a light-reading—simple enough by conversion into an optical track, as is used in film recording. This track was projected in magnification upon a screen and carefully examined by my experts and myself. Each 'peak' and 'valley' of the Voice was carefully measured. It is an accepted fact that anybody's voice when recorded in this manner never produces identical peaks. There are variations all the time, otherwise every natural voice would be without inflection—a flat, cold, robot-like tone...."

"This is interesting, Mr. Gascoyne," the judge put in, "but can you explain who *did* speak? Or how the Voice was created?"

"The Voice," Gascoyne said slowly, "was *drawn*! With painstaking skill and, possibly, a thin mapping pen and Indian ink, the peaks and valleys of a voice were drawn on transparent film, every word being correctly drawn so it would sound, when convened, like the real thing. That is how the richness and basso-profundo quality were achieved. Yes, it was drawn—peak by peak and valley by valley; and then it was presumably run through a normal projector sound-head and recorded onto tape. The whole feat is entirely possible, m'lud, being merely a variation of optical and magnetic sound recording."

"This is preposterous," Martin Shaw was heard to murmur, staring, at which Lennox shot him a triumphant glance. Then he turned back to the judge.

"May I return Albert Simpkins to the stand, m'lud, to clear up the details of this particular matter?"

"If you wish, Mr. Lennox. Thank you, Mr. Gascoyne, for your illuminating evidence...."

In a moment or two Albert had taken Gascoyne's place.

"How much," Lennox asked, "do you confirm of Mr. Gascoyne's findings?"

"All of them," Albert replied promptly. "About a year ago I was a cinema projectionist—and had been one for many years. The science of optics and sound recording fascinated me. I discovered one day that by drawing a haphazard track on a spare piece of film I could produce weird sounds. At that time it was just an interesting bit of tinkering—but the idea grew. How about drawing a voice that nobody had ever owned? I studied the peaks of normal voices, together with the valleys, and made a careful note of the height of the peaks producing corresponding vocal noises. In time

I had roughed out an experimental track and stayed overtime at the cinema to try it out when everybody else had gone home. By this means, and many hours of microscopic work, I finally drew the messages that the Conqueror's Voice later spoke. As Gascoyne said, I drew them on film, ran them through the projector's sound-head as audible speech, and then recorded them back onto a tape recorder. That same Voice spoke to the world."

A heavy silence fell on the court. The Prosecuting Counsel sat down and scowled at his notes.

"I knew the legal position in which I might one day stand," Albert explained. "The law would accuse the Voice of doing the damage proper and maybe link me as an accessory. But no law exists to indict a voice without a body, so on that count no charge can stand. I *can* be charged as the creator of the Voice, but that overrides the charge of 'false pretences.'"

"That," the judge agreed, fingering the top of his nose with painful indecision, "is entirely correct."

"But there remains the fact," Shaw exclaimed, jumping up again, "that the prisoner *did* make the Voice. He *did* send the recordings in a missile. He *did*—"

"Can you prove that the Voice spoke from a missile?" Lennox asked quietly.

"Prove it? *Prove* it? It is common knowledge! Scotland Yard's radar experts pinpointed the missile at a hundred thousand miles distance and—"

"They pinpointed *something*," Lennox corrected,

"but nobody has yet proved that it was a missile. Two men have died in their efforts to get that evidence."

"Douglas Marshall declared that there was such a missile and that he was going to examine it."

"I have here," Lennox said, withdrawing a note from his pocket, "a communication from Mount Palomar Observatory—and with your indulgence, m'lud, I would like the court to hear it. It is dated today at two a.m., and was transmitted direct to me. It says: 'Responding to your urgent legal request, both radar and visual observations have been made of space one-hundred-thousand miles away, approximating the position supposedly containing orbit of remote-controlled missile fired from Earth. No trace of a missile can be detected, either visually or by detectors.' It is possible," Lennox finished, "that a recent mysterious star seen in that vicinity might have been caused by an explosion which blew up the missile. It is equally possible that the gallant gentlemen, Forsythe and Marshall, were deluded when they gave their reports— We are entitled to *assume* whatever we wish, but I submit that we have no *proof* of a missile when one does not exist, and we have no case against a voice because no human possessed it. On that, m'lud, I rest my case insofar as the first part of the indictment is concerned...."

Plainly, the Prosecution had not a leg to stand on, but the second part of the indictment, the murder of Vera Simpkins, was a different matter. Here Martin Shaw had no concrete evidence with which to swing the balance in his client's favor, and desperately though he fought the Prosecution in the ensuing days, he knew he was losing step by step.

The clamor set up by the public was tremendous. Now it had become common knowledge that disarmament and peace had been brought about by one man's ingenuity, there was not—as Albert had secretly expected—a vast wave of vilification in his direction. Quite the contrary! Suddenly he was an idol, the savior of mankind, all that a man should be, and other platitudes too numerous to mention. Indeed, the force of public opinion on his side was so great that it even silenced the aggressive voices of those merchants of death who had piled up fortunes from armaments. They did not dare raise dissenting voices when so many were on the side of the man they sought to attack.

Albert, when he heard of the public reaction, began to hope that this flood of eulogy would sweep him out of the law court to freedom—but Jerome Lennox was under no such illusion. He knew that no matter how hard the public clamored, the juggernaut majesty of the law would continue on its way. As yet Albert Simpkins was an unconvicted murderer. Only one thing could bring him back into the world of freedom: proof that he was innocent.

And apparently this proof was not forthcoming. On the fourth day the laborious trial ended in stifling conditions and the jury retired to consider its verdict. It was absent for two hours and the verdict the foreman gave was immediately flashed to the newspapers and television reports throughout the world. London papers flared with big headlines in the early issues:

SIMPKINS FOUND GUILTY!

BENEFACTOR CONDEMNED
TO LIFE IMPRISONMENT!

The *Evening Globe* was particularly pungent in its leader, demanding to know how the jury had the impudence to find a man totally blameless on the first count, yet completely guilty—with no mitigating circumstances—on the second. The whole trial was declared a farce, a scandal, an example of legal bigotry, and downright viciousness.... But the inexorable fact remained that Albert Simpkins was to be committed in ten days, on the morning of August 20th.

Lennox saw Albert in his remand cell, and demanded that he appeal against the sentence. But to his dismay, his request was met with a determined shake of the head. Albert gave a faint smile and patted the lawyer's arm. "You are a good friend, Jerry, even if you are a legal man," he said dryly. "There are no more possible clues you can find so don't waste your time. You saw how much notice the jury took of your trump card about the trees being burned as well as Vera. Can't blame 'em, I suppose. The average man and woman has little conception of scientific values."

"You maintain that you did not kill your daughter, and I fully believe you. Therefore, somebody else did—or at least, *something* did. I'll sort it out, even if I have to prove there was a wandering flash of lightning which struck her down— But at least give me a chance by letting me appeal for you."

"No." Albert shook his head. "I'd rather finish it."

And in this he was adamant. In nine days he would start his life sentence, and that would end his strange odyssey. From cinema projectionist to master of the world, and from master of the world to convicted murderer—all in not quite two years. He had certainly made up for the long early period when life had been undisturbed by a single arresting incident.

In the outer world the public demand for his reprieve was spreading like a bush fire. Endless petitions were drawn up and signed—not only by the ordinary work-aday men and women but also by really top names, and especially the two doctors to whom genius in medical discovery had been given. Albert Simpkins was not the Almighty, they asserted, but he had most definitely got powers that were denied to the rank and file. Such a man could not be *allowed* to be shut away in a cell. He had too much to give.

All to no avail. Albert Simpkins remained in his cell; the law took no notice of the public demand—and slowly the clamor began to die down. Such news as there was of public behavior reached Albert through Jerome Lennox, who never gave up pleading or working for his client who had become a bosom friend. Somewhere, somehow, Lennox insisted, there had to be the right answer. It was not justice or even common-sense that a man with so much, and declaring himself innocent, should finish being locked away.

* * * * * * *

It was on August 18th, two days before his trans-
portation to the prison where he was to start his
sentence was due, that Albert found himself unexpect-
edly dreaming. He recalled that once before he had
been caught "napping" like this—on that hot summer
evening at the big house he had bought, when he had
sprawled in the armchair whilst Emily had seen to it that
Ethel had her supper. The dream this time was fairly
similar to that other one—a curious sense of drifting
beyond things mundane, of an ethereal bouying up as
though he had been mysteriously cut adrift from things
material. And the odd thing was that he *knew* it was a
dream. He kept telling himself so, and that he would
soon awaken to the dreary gray of his remand cell and
realize that more precious hours had slipped by in the
relentless course of time.

Upon his dream sense there suddenly appeared a spot
of light. To begin with it was only the tiniest speck, but
with extreme rapidity it increased in size until it seemed
to be blazing right through the universe. In the center
of the intolerable haze—which would have destroyed
anything but dream-sight, which was untouchable—
Albert beheld a curious dark nucleus. It was as if there
hovered there, on the edge of the unknowable, a something of blinding electric brilliance which was also
sentient and alive.

Albert, as he lay dreaming on his bunk, could sense
the overpowering waves of electrical energy that were
surging around him, but since they only impinged

against his dream-self, they did him no injury. He felt he was embraced in this titanic aura of brilliance, as though he had become a part of it. It was only the ineradicable power of his own individual will which kept telling him this was a dream, an excursion into the mental realm— And then, a voice! At least it sounded like a voice, yet he knew he did not hear it with his own ears. It was entirely mental and he automatically interpreted it into his own language. A thought and mental vibration are the same thing in *any* language.

"I know you can hear me, O man of Earth. Nor shall I harm you, for you I and my fellows have the greatest affection. You stand as one amongst multimillions who have been given vast power and yet have not abused it."

The light swirled and gyrated and Albert shifted uneasily on his bunk.

"Once before I almost communicated with you, but the contact was broken by the arrival of your wife. You believed that you dreamed, but that was not so. Your mind was projected into the depths of space, to me. I am a being of Andromeda that you, in your puny physical vestment, *pretended to be* in order to make sense out of a chaotic world.... Have no fear, man of Earth. I and my fellows hold no malice against you for having pretended to be a being of Andromeda, but it is right that you should know that your mental waves, in which you expressed the fact that you had come from faraway Andromeda, reached us. We, pure intellectuals, were puzzled. Who could this person, this entity, be who claimed he was one of us? I came to see for myself...."

Albert moved, but he did not waken.

"I, Man of Earth, am as far beyond you in intelligence as you are beyond the worm. I and my fellows take no heed of material laws which postulate distance, time, and space. These laws do not actually exist: they are invented for convenience. We move instantly to wherever we wish—hence my movement from what you call Andromeda to this particular space of yours— was accomplished with the instantaneous swiftness of thought itself. Then it was that I found a Man of Earth who was trying in his small, non-advanced way to bring peace and happiness to his fellows by claiming to be a super-creature from outer space. I returned to my people and we debated the matter. You deserved help in your lone struggle and, with our superior knowledge, we could give it to you. I was given the assignment of seeing that your laudable scheme came to success. We—so long ago it is beyond conception— once brought peace to our own material world in just such a way as you have brought it to yours, hence our reason for wishing to help.

"I realize now, however, that I have perhaps been overzealous in protecting you. My concern was to destroy every hand raised against you. To that end I wiped out the young Earth woman—your daughter— who was about to expose your work to the police. In just the same way I destroyed the man in space who was going to bring back evidence of your missile and the instruments therein. My method of destruction was simple. Normally, we are invisible, but in the need to annihilate a foe we can draw unto ourselves and generate cosmic electro-magnetic energy in ever-mounting voltage without harm to ourselves, because our controlling minds are superior to it. But to a material structure this cosmic energy is annihilating. So then, acting as your constant guardian, I wiped out whatever threatened you, never foreseeing that your own life would be threatened and that you would be blamed, at least insofar as your daughter is concerned...."

"Give me the way out," Albert whispered, struggling between sleep and awakening. "Give—give me the way out...."

"The way out is simple, Man of Earth. As recompense, I shall make it appear that the solution has been entirely conceived by you, which, I trust, will make you an even greater hero amongst your people when you are released. I am going to infuse into your mind certain scientific facts and with them you will gain your release. You will not remember afterwards that I was the giver of your knowledge, nor will you ever contact me again. When I have given you the key to freedom, my task is finished, and I shall return whence I came, satisfied that your ambition to produce a peaceful planet will eventually be realized.... Now listen, Man of Earth, to what I have to tell you...."

CHAPTER ELEVEN

An hour later Albert awoke. He was feeling curiously confused and unaccountably tired. This latter could be explained away by the tremendous drain on his physical reserves entailed by the effort of involuntary concentration. He lay still on his bunk for a long time, thinking, then at last he struggled to his feet and contacted the warder.

"What's the time?" he asked.

"Time? Half-past three in the afternoon. What's the matter? You haven't a train to catch, have you?"

"No, but I must have an interview immediately with my lawyer, and also with the dean of Laboratory 9. It is absolutely essential. Tell the prison governor that those two gentlemen can probably establish my innocence."

The warder shrugged and went on his way, leaving Albert reasonably sure that his request would be granted. It was. The prison governor was as anxious as everybody else to have Albert freed so that he could carry on his good work.

By four o'clock Jerome Lennox and the venerable scientist had arrived, the lawyer in particular looking eager.

"This means you've decided to appeal, doesn't it?" he asked urgently. "There isn't much time, but perhaps I—"

"I'm not appealing. I'm going to provide enough evidence to make a retrial worthwhile, or even an unconditional pardon when the authorities see what I have to offer. You'll attend to the scientific side, Dean, and you the legal, Jerry."

"Willingly!" the lawyer exclaimed.

"Well," Albert said, taking a deep breath, "this is it: I am going to show to the authorities in three-D color exactly what happened to my unhappy daughter."

Lawyer and scientist looked at each other in wonder. Was this the first sign of a man cracking under the strain, or—

"I'm not crazy," Albert said quietly, the two men sitting on the bunk on either side of him. "I think you'll both admit that I have a fair degree of scientific knowledge—and in these past days whilst waiting for the sentence I have also had time to think things out. A brilliant notion has occurred to me and, remotely, it is based on the theory of the Conservation of Energy."

"That's out of my line," Lennox confessed.

"Listen just the same. I'm sure you'll follow me, Dean, at least. Briefly, the Law of Conservation of Energy states that nothing in the Universe can ever be lost, otherwise the Universe itself would fall to pieces. In other words, if matter be destroyed, we get energy, and if we destroy energy—which is less likely—we get matter. Right?"

"Interchangeable states, yes," the Dean agreed. "But what has it to do with your problem?"

"Just this: Since nothing can be destroyed, light waves cannot be destroyed either. Unless some powerful force changes them into a new type of radiation, they remain exactly as created until they dissipate, until their energy becomes uniform with that of the cosmos itself. Correct?"

"It's high-flown," the Dean reflected, "but basically possible. Science postulates that a light wave continues in an outwardly flowing circle of radiation at one hundred and eighty-six thousand miles a second until, as you say, the energy of the wave has spent itself—but in the case of a light wave that cannot be for quite a long period...."

"In other words," Albert said deliberately, "the light waves given off at the death of my daughter are still moving through space! Everything material is only cognized by the light waves it gives of. Travel far enough and recapture waves generated centuries back in the past, and you could exactly reproduce the event in movie form. What I am suggesting is the recapture of the light waves generated immediately before and after my daughter's death, which waves will be reproduced for the authorities to see. Obviously, since the waves will be the originals, shorter or longer according to color, they will reproduce the exact color and detail together with natural three-dimensional depth."

"Er—do you mean by a film projector?" the Dean hazarded.

"No—the real thing! By using the fourth dimension, the actual light-waves overtaken and reproduced. After that we can use the instrument for overtaking the light waves of past events and let the world see what really did happen in the case of unsolved mysteries."

"I see." The Dean looked bothered and waited for the next. The lawyer sat with one eyebrow up and a blank stare, then he demanded:

"And do you seriously aver that this scientific miracle is practical?"

"Certainly it is! Afterwards, science can add the instrument to their achievements, providing I get credit as the inventor. I'm looking to you, Dean, to supervise the engineering side. And there isn't much time, either."

"Not quite forty-eight hours," the Dean said seriously. "Dammit, man, it just can't be done!"

"It can be, and it must be. Technically, the problem is not so complicated as it may appear. The basic principle is that of radio engineering, with special modifications and a great mass of power. The power isn't a problem with atomic energy at your back. I can sketch out the entire design right here and then you can get busy.... Give me some paper, Jerry."

Lennox did so, from his briefcase. He looked like a man in a dream. The Dean for his part sat with his high forehead crinkled as he watched the condemned man drawing rapidly on the paper, his hand moving with the assurance of a draughtsman, never once pausing—and working entirely without instruments or scale-rule.

Half an hour passed. Lawyer and scientist shifted positions to alleviate cramp, but Albert still worked on, lost completely in concentration. So complete was his attention upon his task, he even seemed to have forgotten that the two men were with him—until at length Lennox spoke.

"How in the name of creation do you do it?" he demanded. "I never saw anything like it before! A design which would do credit to a trained engineer whipped off like a doodle on a telephone book! It isn't just scientific genius; it's—well, I'm damned if I know *what* it is."

"Just inspiration." Albert smiled as he glanced up. "Let it go at that. Maybe I'm possessed or something. I wouldn't know. Anyway, Dean, there are the details, design, and general specification. I don't think you'll find I've forgotten anything. If I have, contact the prison governor immediately and he'll allow you to see me."

"And this," the Dean asked, studying the plan and copious notes, "is the whole thing?"

"That's it. Operational instructions are in the margin there. All perfectly simple— Now get busy and build. And you, Jerry, start the ball rolling for the legal preliminaries concerning a new trial."

"Yes, but...." Lennox frowned to himself. "What happens if this fantastic idea of yours doesn't work out?"

"It will. You have nothing to fear on that score. Your grounds for a fresh trial will be that you have obtained—or very soon will obtain—important new evidence vindicating me of the charge brought against me in regard to my daughter's death. Do what you can. You understand the law: I don't."

Albert's confidence was so infectious that both Lennox and the Dean believed him in spite of themselves. So they took their departure, and for Albert there was nothing left but to wait—and indeed to wonder more than somewhat at the amazing thing he had accomplished. He had no memory of the manner in which his evanescent genius had been given to him. The thought of a being from Andromeda never even occurred to him. From his point of view it simply seemed that Providence had come to his aid with a particularly brilliant idea.

And, in the outer world, the Dean went to work. He used his considerable influence to get the finest scientific engineers to work on the plan. Some of them vaguely understood it, others not at all—but since in general it was so brilliantly executed, they could hardly go wrong. And, hour after hour, different departments of the country's engineering resources saw some particular part of the strange instrument form under their hands. Immediately a part was finished it was flown to Laboratory 9, there to await incorporation into other parts.

So finally, by noon the following day, the apparatus was complete. It stood four feet high and looked rather like a conventional radio-television cabinet, but within it were complicated contrivances, the like of which science had never seen before. For power it used atomic energy, generating such a high voltage that the operators in the immediate neighborhood considered it safer to wear insulated clothing.

The news of the machine's completion was immediately sent to Albert, Lennox himself being the bearer of the glad tidings.

"Has it been tested?" Albert asked quickly, and Lennox shook his head.

"Not yet. The Dean thought it better to inquire of you first what must be done."

"All that is necessary is to release the master-button, clearly shown in the plan, and the machine will do the rest. It will send forth a magnetic radiation into space via the fourth dimension—thereby foreshortening space and exceeding the speed of light, in order to catch up with the outflowing waves. By a process of mathematics and electronics—too complicated for your legal mind, I'm afraid—it will automatically be attracted by the particular frequency of light waves we are seeking. When that happens, the light waves thus trapped will be redirected back along the original fourth-dimensional beam—again at supra-light speed. The transformers will interpret the incoming radiations, and upon the screen of the instrument there will appear—after the fashion of television—a complete light-picture of what really happened to my poor daughter."

"Oh!" Lennox was trying hard to understand. "I only hope the judge and jury will accept this glorified television as evidence in the legal sense."

"They will have to, because nothing else but super-science will be able to explain how the picture has been contrived.... What I would suggest," Albert finished, "is that you explain to the law the exceptional circumstances—that my sentence is fixed for eight tomorrow morning—and have a retrial convened for this evening."

"I'll do my best," Lennox promised. "Be a matter of getting round Judge Hanbury, but he's a humane old devil when it comes to it."

So again Albert had to wait, but behind the scenes Lennox did not waste a moment, or any of his persuasive power. To convince Judge Hanbury of the need of the retrial was not easy, but finally—because a man's quality of life depended on it—the judge agreed. A jury was summoned in record time by special order, and the tip-off to the media resulted in the early evening papers and radio and television news being full of the sudden sensational developments. Emily listened to and read of these intended happenings, and vaguely wondered what her husband had done this time. Up to this point she had been quite convinced that his sentence was inevitable. So she promptly made tracks for the High Court of Justice, and left Ethel to look after the younger children.

By seven o'clock that evening the rush and hurry was over. The jury took its place, the counsels were present, and the judge—looking vaguely suspicious—was awaiting a miracle. That there would be trouble if one was not forthcoming he had already made abundantly clear to the still uneasy Lennox.

Dominating the floor of the court, before the counsels' table and judge's bench, was the remarkable instrument upon which Albert was pinning all his hopes. Beside it, in radiation-proof suits, stood the Dean of Laboratory 9 and one assistant.

"You will be good enough, Mr. Lennox, to state the nature of the new evidence you have to offer," the judge said at length. "And I must ask you not to waste the court's time unduly. It has already been extremely inconvenient to convene a court at this hour.... Proceed."

"M'lud, I find myself at a loss," Lennox confessed. "The evidence about to be presented is not so much mine as that of my client. Everything relies on this—er—equipment you see standing here. With your permission, I would prefer my client to explain things for himself."

"Permission granted." The judge was obviously out of patience with the whole business. "The prisoner may proceed."

From where he stood between the two guardian warders Albert began speaking. Everybody listened intently, including Emily. And the more she heard, the more she realized that her incurable husband had again pulled one of his wizardry stunts out of the bag.

"You behold here, m'lud, a scientific instrument expressly designed by me. I shall not weary you or the court with the scientific details, but I do call upon the Dean of Laboratory 9—who is standing there beside the machine, in an insulated suit—to corroborate that the invention *is* entirely mine and that I stand or fall by what it does."

"Well, what *does* it do?" the judge snapped, after a brief glance at the Dean's head nodding inside the helmet.

"It reproduces the light waves of a time past, m'lud. In this instance it will show on the screen exactly what happened when my daughter met her death, of whose murder I have been accused."

"Ridiculous!" Martin Shaw cried, leaping up. "M'lud, if this is the kind of idiocy to which we are to be subjected, I beg leave—"

"Mr. Shaw, I no more concur with this irregular procedure than you do," the judge interrupted, "but I would have you bear in mind that the prisoner is fighting for his freedom and reputation, and therefore it is up to us to bear with him in the presentation of this new evidence—if such it is."

"That being so," Albert said quietly, "I will not waste any more time on details: those can be given afterwards. I would ask that the court be cleared for an area of nine feet around the projector so as to prevent harm from any stray radiation."

"Let that be done," the judge ordered, and the clerk saw to it that it was; In a matter of five minutes the court was cleared within the prescribed limits and every eye became fixed on the apparatus as, at a nod from Albert, the Dean moved the master-switch, his assistant meanwhile keeping an eye on the complicated control panel.

Numerous "magic eye" windows began to glow with varicolored lights. The only sound was a faint humming. The spectators hardly moved. The members of the Press and other media hovered near the doors of the courtroom, waiting to hurl themselves outside report the biggest story in legal history. Here was sensation and scientific magic in the making, and the only man who understood the details was Albert himself—tense, his forehead moist, his fists clenched. That solitary screen in the center of the projector seemed abominably dark and unresponsive. Those seated at the rear of the instrument shifted restlessly, jealous of their more fortunate fellows

"It may take a little while," came Albert's voice, in the aching silence. "We have to remember that, by now, the original light waves have traveled several light-weeks, and have to be overtaken and recaptured."

Since hardly anybody understood what he was talking about, there was no comment, not even from the judge. Minutes dragged on. Albert knew that if something did not happen quickly the judge would clear the court, fume at the failure to produce evidence, and that would be that— Then, abruptly, the screen glowed with silvery light, just as an old-fashioned television screen might have looked with the power warming up. There came a sigh of relief and murmurs of expectancy.

"Dim the lights!" the judge ordered—and half of them were extinguished. Although there was still mellow evening light outside, the shadows of neighboring buildings made the courtroom gloomy and cheerless.

Gradually the screen came into full relief and Albert drew a deep, trembling sigh. There, clearly depicted, was Vera on the seat in the recreation ground, just as though a camera were trained upon her from perhaps twenty feet away. Close to her was the lake, the small "swan island" in its center, bushes sprouting thereon. Nor was this all. The view shifted a little and there came in sight none other than Albert himself, seated on a seat at the other side of the lake, his "box of tricks" beside him, his hat pushed up on his forehead

"You can see by that that I am not involved in the business," came Albert's voice out of the gloom. "Not at any time did I— Ah!" he broke off tensely. "I believe, m'lud, that here we have the explanation!"

As Albert had spoken, an intensely bright light had formed over the lake on the side nearest Vera. Further away, Albert was still settled, unconcerned, on the seat. Then Vera sprang to her feet as the light phenomenon became larger, simultaneously moving towards her. She started running— Then she fell dead, arms out flung, her handbag bouncing away across the grass. And there she remained until a park ranger came into view and hurried towards her.... And, on his own seat, Albert yawned and contemplated the sky.

"Stop the machine!" Albert called, and the Dean obeyed.

The lights returned. Those in the courtroom looked at each other. Emily, who had had a good view, had hidden her face in her handkerchief, only just able to control herself at having witnessed in so stark a fashion the death of her eldest child.

"Well, m'lud?" Albert asked gravely, looking at him.

The judge hesitated. For the first time in his long and learned career he had been caught on one foot.

"I do not profess to know," he said slowly, "by what scientific process this demonstration has been made, but I most certainly congratulate the inventor. Whilst watching that most harrowing scene I kept thinking that here was either live television or a televised film, until I realized such a thing could not possibly be. If it had been a film, the girl would have been aware of the camera and, at some point—since she was not an actress, nor collaborating in any way—would have glanced towards it. On the other hand, it could not be live television, because we have seen something which we know happened a long time ago...."

The judge cleared his throat and it was plain he was wondering if he was making sense. Finally he looked towards the jury.

"Ladies and gentlemen of the jury, the demonstration you have witnessed is, of course, quite without precedent, but I instruct you to remember that throughout the projection we saw the prisoner seated at the opposite side of the lake, entirely at peace with the world. He was not operating the instrument beside him, nor was he apparently aware of the proximity of his daughter. By no stretch of imagination can we call the scene we have just witnessed a clever fake. It was not that. It was the real thing, mysteriously recaptured from the past by the genius of this man whom we, adhering to law, have had to accuse of murder. You will consider your verdict in view of this new evidence and—"

"If I may say so, m'lud," the foreman interposed, rising, "we are all agreed without need of retirement. We find the prisoner not guilty on all counts...."

ABOUT THE AUTHOR

British writer JOHN RUSSELL FEARN was born near Manchester, England, in 1908. As a child he devoured the science fiction of Wells and Verne, and was a voracious reader of the Boys' Story Papers. He was also fascinated by the cinema, and first broke into print in 1931 with a series of articles in *Film Weekly*.

He then quickly sold his first novel, *The Intelligence Gigantic*, to the American magazine, *Amazing Stories*. Over the next fifteen years, writing under several pseudonyms, Fearn became one of the most prolific contributors to all of the leading US science fiction pulps, including such legendary publications as *Astounding Stories*, *Startling Stories*, *Thrilling Wonder Stories*, and *Weird Tales*.

During the late 1940s he diversified into writing novels for the UK market, and also created his famous superwoman character, The Golden Amazon, for the prestigious Canadian magazine, the Toronto *Star Weekly*. In the early 1950s in the UK, his fifty-two novels as "Vargo Statten" were bestsellers, most notably his novelization of the film, *Creature from the Black Lagoon*.

Apart from science fiction, he had equal success with westerns, romances, and detective fiction, writing an amazing total of 180 novels—most of them in a period of just ten years—before his early death in 1960. His work has been translated into nine languages, and continues to be reprinted and read worldwide.

www.ingramcontent.com/pod-product-compliance
Lightning Source LLC
Chambersburg PA
CBHW031420250626
47155CB00004B/1557